T0072505

Shadows and Secrets of the
DuPris Cottage

*A Fictional Narrative of One Woman's Life, the
Legacy She Left Behind, Based on Historical
Events, and the Author's Memories*

Cathy De Anne

BALBOA.
PRESS
A DIVISION OF HAY HOUSE

I have created this work of fiction to honor the memory of my great grandmother. It is a fictional account of her life and those who were part of it. The narrative contains several historical facts, which are part of the public domain, as well as many personal memories of the author's experiences while growing up in her great grandmother's boarding house. These are all part of the story along with events and places from the author's creative imagination. Certain events and stories are fiction. Many factual events and stories were related to me by my grandmother and grandfather (my great-grandmother's son), and are very much a part of the entire work. I have tried to recreate events, locales and conversations of a fictional nature. In order to maintain the anonymity of family members, I have changed the names of all the characters and geographical locations. I also may have changed some identifying characteristics and details such as physical properties, occupations and places of residence. Any resemblance to actual persons living or dead or actual events is purely coincidental. Facts, fiction, memories, stories from the past and the author's imagination have been woven throughout the pages of the book.

Balboa Press books may be ordered through booksellers or by contacting:

Balboa Press
A Division of Hay House
1663 Liberty Drive
Bloomington, IN 47403
www.balboapress.com
1 (877) 407-4847

Because of the dynamic nature of the Internet, any web addresses or links contained in this book may have changed since publication and may no longer be valid. The views expressed in this work are solely those of the author and do not necessarily reflect the views of the publisher, and the publisher hereby disclaims any responsibility for them.

The author of this book does not dispense medical advice or prescribe the use of any technique as a form of treatment for physical, emotional, or medical problems without the advice of a physician, either directly or indirectly. The intent of the author is only to offer information of a general nature to help you in your quest for emotional and spiritual well-being. In the event you use any of the information in this book for yourself, which is your constitutional right, the author and the publisher assume no responsibility for your actions.

Any people depicted in stock imagery provided by Thinkstock are models, and such images are being used for illustrative purposes only. Certain stock imagery © Thinkstock.

Print information available on the last page.

ISBN: 978-1-5043-4316-9 (sc)
ISBN: 978-1-5043-4317-6 (e)

Balboa Press rev. date: 10/26/2015

Dedication

For My Daughter Jeanene and
My Beloved Parents

Acknowledgements

Thank you to my daughter, Jeanene Elizabeth Hamaker for her excellent and time-consuming research of the historical facts.

Special thanks to Martha Burkhart-Cawley for her valued knowledge in assisting me in the editing and completion of the manuscript.

A heartfelt thank you to all others who have, in any way contributed to writing of this book.

Introduction - 2009

I entered my driveway and parked the car. As I approached the front door, I heard the phone ringing. Quickly inserting the key in the door, I hoped I would not miss the call. Picking up the phone but before I could even say hello, I heard this loud voice, "Mom, Mom, do you know the real true story of your great grandmother, Jane DuPris?"

Victoria, her voice at the height of excitement said, "You are not going to believe some of the information that I just discovered!" Before I tell you, how much do you remember about your years growing up in the big house?

For a brief moment, I recalled that during the war years I lived with my parent's and two brothers on an island, in a large old Victorian home owned by my grandparents. Always known to the family as the "big house", it was located on an island off the coast of Maine. There were numerous conversations around the dinner table about my grandfather's mother, Jane DuPris. Nevertheless, I was never privy to all the personal events of her life.

Excitedly, Victoria continued to explain how while researching our family history on my mother's side, she was led to information about an old Victorian home, known as the DuPris Cottage that still stands on the island. It revealed that the house had once belonged to the Simpson-Camden family. I knew that was my mom's family name, and DuPris was my great grandmother's maiden name, so it had to be the big house where our family all lived together throughout the years of World War II. Victoria's question suddenly propelled me into memories of the past, somewhere lost in time. However, they were insisting that the big house and the DuPris Cottage were one in the same. Learning what Victoria had uncovered, sent me back to another time in my life. Attempting to recall events from sixty years earlier, the only thing that came to mind was that the house was to be demolished to make way for some new type of housing. It seemed a lifetime ago since I had thought, in any depth, about my early life as a little girl, and the years I spent in that house.

Following the difficult and challenging period of World War II, my dad, Jack Cole had finally settled into a good paying position for several years, as an engineer. In 1952, my parents decided to buy a home of their own on the mainland for our immediate family. We moved from the big house where my grandmother Mary, my grandfather William and Mary's sister, Iris remained. Almost a year later in March of 1953 my grandfather suddenly passed away. Not long after the funeral, the state sent my grandmother a certified letter offering to purchase his estate, which included the house, a bungalow and a store, in order to build some type of government housing. The offer came at the right time since my grandmother, now a widow in her seventies, sadly knew that she and her older sister, who had never married, were no longer able to care for the property.

The passage of time changes so many things in a family and my mom decided it was now our turn to provide a place for her mother, Mary and Aunt Iris to live out their golden years. Shortly after that our family, once again, were all living under one roof. The years went by and we never thought much more about the fate of the big house. We never returned to the island.

Several years later, my grandmother Mary received word through a friend who still lived on the island that the government's plans never came to fruition. Instead, the local historical society had purchased the house from the state. They wanted to preserve the rich history that the island experienced during its hay day. In addition, my great grandmother Jane DuPris, along with her scandalous story and the DuPris Cottage, were all very much a part of that history.

Recently, as Victoria began to investigate more of our history and that of the house, she learned that not having the funds to refurbish it, the historical society eventually turned it back over to the local town government. For many years, without our knowledge, it remained vacant and uncared for. The town was not sure what to do with it. After some additional research, Victoria learned that the property was very rundown and was up for sale. If there were no interested purchasers after a reasonable time it would eventually be demolished.

Researching back to the late 1800's Victoria uncovered a brief history of the events surrounding the DuPris Cottage, how my great grandmother came to own it and the great improprieties in her life that always seemed to turn up in the local newspapers. Tenaciously Victoria delved into the life and legacy of Jane DuPris through numerous newspaper articles and ancestry records. She also had available to her, my memories, burial records and the deed to my grandfather's and great-grandmother's grave, left to the family by my grandmother, Mary who lays next to her beloved husband William. That discovery resulted in teaching me, and my daughter, about a strong-willed, self-sufficient woman who came long before us. It is the life story and legacy of one courageous, hard-working, determined woman, and those of us who came after her. I was not aware of all the events that had shaped the life of my great grandmother, Jane DuPris, on that island so long ago, but I was soon to find out.

Prologue

In the early spring of 2010, my daughter Victoria and her family were packing for an extended vacation to an island in the northeast. Still a popular destination for the wealthy, the island had many resorts and hotels, but only a few Bed & Breakfast Inns. When Victoria learned that the DuPris Cottage had been part of her family history, her curiosity became the impetus that was to create a major life-change direction for all concerned. Learning that the house was for sale, she convinced her husband Eddie to take a trip and look the place over. Eddie, not knowing what Victoria really had in mind, went cheerfully along with the idea. Upon arrival on the island, they stopped to ask directions.

The DuPris Cottage, once a part of my great grandmother's estate, was located on a large piece of property. Sitting high on a hill overlooking the ocean, with an absolutely, breathtaking view, this lovely Victorian home built in 1892 was very well known to all the islanders. When Victoria viewed it for the first time, she was awe-struck by the beauty of the location, and immediately knew what she was determined to do. From all that she discovered about Jane DuPris and her life, Victoria intuitively knew in her heart that she would heartily agree with her plan.

Still beautiful with white sandy beaches the island has a spectacular shoreline. Part of the coast is rocky and picturesque. Back in the late 1800's the fishing industry provided a thriving livelihood for the locals. The island had a small population that grew profusely during the summer months. In earlier times, it was a haven for fisherman, with beach cottages and an old run down building, that at one time had been a hotel. Air conditioning, not yet in fashion, and as the hot summer season approached, people looked to escape the sizzling oppressive heat of the cities along the eastern seaboard. With delightfully balmy ocean breezes from the Atlantic, the island created the perfect getaway. The climate became the incentive for attracting hordes of summer tourists from those same cities. Along with the travelers came businessmen, adventurers and visionaries. Looking to the future, they began planning how this island paradise could become a mecca for tourists vacationing from the mainland. They purchased land and began to build resort hotels, and inns that eventually became boarding houses. During the summer season, it soon became a favorite vacation spot for ordinary folks, the wealthy, and sometimes the corrupt.

Victoria, a visionary in her own way, and now aware of some of our family history from my many memories of the past, knew at that very moment absolutely no one else would buy or own the house except our family. In addition, she certainly was not about to allow it to be destroyed.

Descending upon the household like a tsunami, this new venture turned their lives upside down. Victoria became obsessed with the fact that somehow she had to have a hand in preserving that house. Knowing Victoria as I do, when she wants something, she will pursue it until she accomplishes it. Her mind, inundated with ideas about the house, she would not let it go.

During a recent visit, I sat in her kitchen having tea and witnessed a very serious discussion about the house between her and her husband. Her mind, it seemed, overtaken with some great fantasy, she was determined to make a reality.

Suddenly, she mumbled, "Why don't we buy it and turn it into a B&B?"

Almost choking as he swallowed his next sip of tea, Eddie blurted out, "What did you say?"

"Oh, I was just thinking out loud, but what do you think about us buying it, restoring it and running as a B & B during the summer?"

"Are you crazy, he blurted out, we live in Georgia?

"Now just listen for a minute and hear me out. Today, the island still attracts tourists from all over and is bustling with activity during the summer months. Owning it would give us the opportunity to live in a different location for the summer months, and it would provide income. I can take an extended summer vacation from work and run it. The income will provide for us all summer. You work out of the house so you can set up a small office there for a couple of months. Maine has a short summer season and it will be a lot cooler than Georgia is, at that time of the year. Besides, the kids will love it".

With all that heated conversation, I decided to go home and let them battle it out without my interference.

For the next week, I was busy with my own life. Then one day the phone rang again.

"Hi Mom, I want to give you an update on a decision we have come to".

Her next words were like an earthquake under my feet.

"We went back to the island and bought the DuPris Cottage. It needs lots of TLC but it will be beautiful when we are finished refurbishing and updating it. We have hired a general contractor and a decorator. They are currently restoring the Cottage and it will be ready by the summer. How would you like to join us there for the first summer season?"

"Hold on, I think I might have to sit down for this!"

After hours of negotiation, Victoria and Eddie finally became the proud owners of a historical 100 year-old Victorian home, where I had grown up.

Restored to perfection, we (me included) would now be spending summers, through some twist of fate, at the DuPris Cottage that had been my childhood home. Wow, to own a B&B had always been one of my secret dreams, and now it was coming true. I could be part of it without any of the major responsibility. Nevertheless, I never dreamed it would manifest in a way that would be taking me back to the home where I had spent so many memorable years as a child.

Renovations almost complete, the DuPris Cottage will open for the summer season and the tourists. We will move into the adjacent bungalow, and it will be the family's summer residence. The small store will house all the supplies needed to run the business.

Returning to my childhood home will take me on a journey of historical events, memories and some very unusual mystical moments...a journey that will stay with me until the end of my days.

Part One

Jane

Out of the past come memories. What was banal, forbidden and sometimes vulgar to one generation is most often transformed by the passage of time to a position that is, acceptable and perhaps sometimes even magical!

Chapter I

Jane & Jonathan

Now in my seventieth year, as I go through the DuPris cottage for the first time since I was 13, I arrive in a euphoric state of nostalgia and memories from my past. Entering the parlor, now redecorated with a lovely Victorian ambiance, I settle into the old rocker that was once my grandmother's favorite chair. Knowing some of the facts about the life of Jane DuPris, my memories begin to take over and to conjure up all the shadows of the past. It propels me into a state of real memories, some facts and a bit of imaginary fantasy. Gazing for a long time at a photo of Jane, and suddenly swept into a dream-like state; the photo of an old woman is now a young girl. I begin to imagine what the island was like back then. Trying to visualize just what her life might have been like, living with her mother on a farm. According to some of the things we discovered, I begin to picture young Jane who is becoming a woman, and in her innocence, has her first experience with a man...

1873

As 1870 approached, the year round population on the island had grown to more than 2000 inhabitants. During the summer season, many visitors from other parts of the northeast came to the island to vacation. The air was pure, and the balmy ocean breezes made it the perfect escape for folks who spent their days in extreme heat, in the many busy cities in the northeast. Wealthy families and successful businesspeople also came, some not as reputable as others.

One visionary, builder and businessperson became an upstanding and notable member of the local community. A successful entrepreneur, he eventually built or purchased hotels, inns and boarding houses on the island and became a well-known and respected member of the community. He was a kind and gentle man of great character. His life will eventually become inter-twined with Jane's in ways that neither of them could have anticipated.

Jane

In a small village in Maine in January of 1856, Bedelia Corning married Raymond DuPris. Ten months later Bedelia gave birth to a baby girl, they named Jane. They resided on a farm along with their two other children. The DuPris' lineage dates back over 100 years in this area. Raymond DuPris died at an early age after a long illness. A young widow with three children under the age of four, Bedelia had no means of support. About a year later, she married a local widower, many years older. The marriage, one of convenience, provided very well for Jane and the other children. A hard working and peaceful family life created a balanced and secure atmosphere for all of them, especially for Jane, over the next several years.

At 17, Jane was not a beauty or the type of young girl that turned heads. In fact, she was rather plain looking with dirty blond hair and brown eyes. Having been through some difficult years growing up, she had learned at an early age to be very independent and self-reliant, with a great determined spirit. Young men she met were not always at ease with her strong independent attitude. However, she had a quick wit and a sensuality about her that seemed to attract and challenge many of them, so she did not lack for the attention of men.

Jane loved to have a good time. She was very bold and flirted with the local men, whenever the right opportunity presented itself. As she matured, she was very aware of her own sexuality, and how easily she attracted the opposite sex, and on some occasions, perhaps the wrong kind. These urges troubled her from time to time but she managed to keep them in check until, she encountered Jonathan Simpson.

Jonathan

Jonathan was born in 1851 in Boston the son of Albert Simpson and Mary Rumple Meyer. Albert supported his family as a seaman. Mary's ancestors were early settlers during revolutionary times. One of them dates back to the 1700's and was a translator for the American Natives, in the days prior to the revolutionary war for independence. Jonathan's family left Boston and moved to

Maine in 1870. He and his siblings became laborers. They found employment in the construction industry that was changing the face of Maine and New Hampshire, and the surrounding areas at the time.

Known for having a bit of a lazy streak, Jonathan seemed unsatisfied with life. Engaged in the chores of the construction industry he seemed burdened and disoriented by manual labor. Coming from a seafaring family, his heart would always lead him back to the fishing industry and the sea. Nevertheless, for some unknown reason he eventually found employment in law enforcement. Having a penchant for manipulation, intimidation and control, this seemed to be the ideal career choice. He liked the feeling of power it gave him, which tended to override his own feelings of inadequacy.

As a teenager, he had been a bully and quite troublesome. As he matured, his attention was always on the local girls more than on his career. His reputation for getting into fights and brawls followed him everywhere. Handsome and charming when he needed to be, with dark curly hair and penetrating blue eyes that twinkled and melted the girls into submission. Jonathan lived in one of the local boarding houses and spent his leisure time at the local pubs. Drinking, fighting and trying to seduce every girl he encountered, seemed to monopolize much of his time. He was not what you would call an ideal choice for a mate nor was he a respected member of the community. Yet, as a deputy in the local sheriff's office and with a huge ego, he always seemed to manage circumstances to his benefit. He was determined to never take no for an answer no matter what the circumstances.

Chapter 2

Their Story

It was July 4 1873, and the small village where they resided on the mainland was bustling with festivities, celebrating U.S. independence. There was dancing at the gazebo in the village square, and the band was playing all the popular romantic songs of the day. Jane, looking her best, was all dressed in a flattering shade of yellow with her hair pulled back away from her face. She was sitting with friends when a young and very good-looking young man approached her and asked her to dance. Since he had quite a reputation in the village, she knew who he was. With that information and the limited wisdom of a 17 year old, she really did not intend to dance with him. She tried to ignore him, but he was very persistent. She looked at him, and then made a wise crack under her breath to her friends. Noticing her unfriendly demeanor, and without waiting for her to answer, he unexpectedly grabbed her hand and yanked her onto the dance floor. Jane was angry and was unable to free herself from his grip. While he whirled her around for several measures of music, she suddenly began to feel very dizzy. Then, all at once, she stopped him in the middle of the floor, politely excused herself and began to walk away.

"Don't you dare leave me standing here", Jonathan demanded.

Quite unsteady on her feet and vertigo controlling her movements she continued to stumble away laughing, and vehemently stated, "I did not agree to dance with you!" Jonathan, now infuriated, immediately followed her and grabbed her by the hand. She, once again, attempted to escape his grip without success, but the song ended and the music suddenly stopped. Immediately pulling her hand out of his, her dizziness now subsided she briskly walked away. Feeling somewhat defeated he returned to where he had been sitting with some friends, who were now whispering and laughing about the incident. Jonathan never let a woman get the best of him so the defeat he felt was only temporary. He immediately began to plan his next move.

Used to always getting his way with women, and as thoughts went racing through his mind, he stated flatly to his friends, "She will not get away with this. Before the night's out she will be dancing with me, and loving it!"

Calming down somewhat from his irritation with Jane, he managed to change his behavior and demeanor. He was an expert at turning on the charm, especially when it became necessary to manipulate a woman. Several dances came and went and soon he was at her side once again. However, this time, charming and poised like a perfect gentleman, he very politely asked, "Miss Jane DuPris, would you do me the honor of dancing with me?" She had her own plan, and winked at one of her friends and sarcastically replied, "Why, I would be delighted!" Jonathan did not miss anything and took note of her sarcasm.

She was actually surprised at her own response and, for the moment, thought about changing her mind. Unfortunately, it was too late and besides, Jane loved a challenge. Looking at him she thought, "He is very attractive and I am really taken with those eyes." Curiosity and the challenge had replaced her original good judgment.

Jane still somewhat naïve, and totally forgetting her initial gut feeling about him, was beginning to let down her defenses. His transformation in attitude seemed to get her attention and his eyes had captivated her from the very moment she first looked into them. When both their eyes finally met on the dance floor, she felt a strange and intense attraction.

As the night's festivities ended, Jane walked home alone remembering the events of the evening. Her thoughts wandered back to Jonathan and how he had manipulated her. She could not believe that she had allowed him to do it.

Thinking as she scolded herself, "Where was that independence and self-assuredness that you are so proud of, Jane DuPris?"

"Oh well, just another guy with a huge ego," came surprisingly out of her mouth, and she dismissed the entire incident. At home, where she lived with her mother, she got into bed and drifted off into a sound sleep.

During the weeks that followed, Jonathan was relentless in his pursuit of her and seemed to show up everywhere she went. Nevertheless, she constantly rebuffed his attention. Then one evening as she was strolling through the woods near her home he suddenly appeared and startled her.

"What do you want?" she asked, and in a very unfriendly tone, demanded, "Please leave me alone!"

As he engaged her in a conversation, she soon began to relax somewhat. Being younger and inexperienced, once again, his charm seemed to be lessening her original reluctance. Looking directly at him, she thought, "he is so handsome, and those eyes are intoxicating." Something was stirring in her and she was beginning to weaken. As they continued to walk and chat about the events of the day, she felt her heart softening toward him. Some subtle sexual feelings that she had felt on earlier occasions in her life were surfacing and disturbing her. More mature now, this time it was different and they seemed more intense. Before they parted he abruptly asked, "Would you like to go out for the evening tomorrow night?" With an overwhelming sense of curiosity, she surprised herself again and shyly accepted, but with some feelings of hesitancy. It is always very flattering when a man pursues you in that way. She was young, innocent and very flattered. Slowly but most unfortunate for Jane, she was succumbing to his manipulation and falling into his clutches.

Still with some feelings of caution as the next evening arrived, she anxiously awaited his arrival, while sitting on the front porch with her mother. Bedelia, now a widow for the third time lived with Jane and two of her other children. Surviving three husbands, she too, was a strong determined woman.

"How much do you know about this young man, Jane?" "Not too much, Mom, but I am curious about him, and seem to find him quite attractive." During the weeks since we met at the dance in town, he has continuously pursued me." Bedelia, somewhat concerned said, "At times like these that I wish your father could be here to help me guide you."

Jonathan arrived on time and Jane introduced the two of them. After a brief exchange of niceties, Jane and Jonathan stepped off the porch, turned and waved good night to her mother. They strolled into town and spent most of the evening at the local sweet shop just talking and getting to know each other. Jane was still under age so a local pub was out of the question.

As the evening progressed, Jane still seemed to have some uncertainty about Jonathan, something intuitive or even a premonition, perhaps. Nevertheless the physical attraction was becoming so strong she somehow knew deep within herself that if the right circumstances presented themselves she might not be able to resist him. Intrigued and challenged by her strong and independent personality, Jonathan wanted her even more. Little did they anticipate what the future had in store for them?

After several dates, the chemistry between them had become extremely intense. He always kissed her good night and she reciprocated. Being a typical 24 year old with a questionable reputation, he was intent on moving their relationship toward some type of intimacy. Still innocent, she was not prepared for that. Still very cautious and trying to keep things under control, she continuously endeavored to maintain somewhat of a distance, without success. Then one night while out for the evening they decided to go for a walk on the beach where he knew it was very secluded and they could be completely alone. The night was cool and scented with the aroma of fall. The moon was full and glistening on the water. You could hear the sound of gentle waves as they rolled to the shore. Jane could feel a soft breeze against her face and the trees were rustling in the wind. The mood was enchanting and made it a perfect romantic setting. Jonathan was very clever and knew exactly what he was doing.

Jane, in her innocence and so captivated by him now, was not consciously aware of how much he was maneuvering her toward a seduction. She looked exceptionally pretty that night. Her pink organdy dress pulled in at the waist accentuated her figure and her dirty blond hair pulled back and tied with a pink satin ribbon looked stunning. He could not take his eyes off her. Jonathan took off his jacket, spread it on the sand and invited her to sit down. Her heart was starting to beat faster now feeling that something new was about to happen. She was scared, nervous and excited all at once. Sitting down beside her, he put his arm around her shoulders and she looked at him. Gazing into his eyes she knew if he kissed her at that moment, she would no longer be able to resist him. He leaned closer to her, pulled her close and kissed her passionately. Without hesitation, she kissed him back with just as much passion. The kiss was long and delicious for them both. As they embraced each other, Jonathan began to unbutton her dress. Her heart beating even faster now, but she did nothing to stop him. Her feelings of passion and excitement were rendering her helpless. In a matter of minutes, as he was fondling her breast, suddenly they were undressing each other. Her sexual urges now at their peak, her longing for him became insatiable and before she knew it, they were making love. He was an experienced lover and knew exactly what he was doing, but this was her first sexual experience. His actual penetration of her was somewhat uncomfortable but she was so aroused that it did not seem to bother her.

As the intenseness of their lovemaking subsided, they lay on the beach for about an hour enveloped in each other's arms not wanting to part. It was these tender moments of first love, which remained in Jane's heart always.

Jane had a curfew and she knew they had better go. As they arrived at her front door they kissed, she went inside and waved to him. Watching him as he walked away down the path to town her mind was racing. All she could think about was what had happened between them just moments ago. Suddenly waves of guilt overcame her. She considered avoiding him during the next few days, but that soon passed as the excitement she felt overrode any feelings of regret.

Lying in bed, she kept going over and over all the events of the evening. Jane could not sleep at all that night, or the next night. She pinched herself to see if it had all been just a dream but she was wide-awake, and realized it had been very real. Thoughts of when they might be together once again consumed her. She spent most of her days just looking forward to the next time she would see him. Over the next few weeks, they spent every spare moment together. Inexperienced, with her hormones now raging, their lovemaking became almost an obsession for them both.

Jane constantly made up stories to her mother so she and Jonathan could be alone. In such a small village, there were not too many places to hide where they would be unnoticed. With lovemaking always a priority, they found secret places where they could rendezvous. Many times, they would return to where they first became intimate. It was the safest place where they could go unobserved, and it held a lovely memory.

They had a brief but intense, and very sexual courtship He was in the process of resigning his position at the police department and becoming a commercial fisherman by trade. However, he always maintained his connection with all the local sheriffs, realizing that might be a huge benefit one day.

Chapter 3

2010

Victoria was frantically calling, "Mom, where are you?" "I'm in here Victoria, in the parlor, looking at Jane's photo," Amanda replied. "You have been gone so long we were beginning to worry what happened to you."

With a deep sigh Amanda said, "From the facts I know about Jane's life, I was just trying to imagine what kind of a life Jane had back in 1873." "So what did you come up with?" "Oh, it was mostly blending what I know with a lot of fantasizing, I think."

"Mom, it's almost dinner time and I thought you might like to make your famous salad."

"Sure, Amanda said, I would love to. Let's do it!"

Dinner turned out lovely. Victoria and Amanda did all the dishes. The kids went outside to play, Eddie and Victoria took their evening walk, but Amanda decided to do more investigating on the second floor.

She climbed the stairs enveloped in her memories. The staircase, the wood, the hall and everyone's bedroom… they were all just as she remembered them. At the end of the hall, there was a lavatory and another room with a sink and a tub. The first room at the top of the stairs had been her parent's bedroom. As she approached, her heart began to beat faster and her hands became sweaty. Something told her that she was not yet ready to enter that room. Recalling a powerful memory, she moved quickly by and continued down the hall. Just as if it was yesterday, she was able to place each family member, in his or her respective bedroom. She was enchanted as she admired the new décor in each room and the restoration reflecting an earlier time in history.

When Victoria and Eddie returned from their evening stroll, they could not find Amanda.

"Now where is she?" Victoria grumbled

"Stop worrying, she will turn up. She is probably just investigating," Eddie retorted. "After all, this is like a walk down memory lane for her."

Victoria quickly responded, "Well I am going up stairs to see if she got lost in the past somewhere!"

Arriving at the top of the stairs Victoria peered into that first room thinking she might find her there, but she was not there. Hearing footsteps Amanda regained her awareness of the present. "I am in what used to be my grandmother's room, Amanda blurted out. If you had come up sooner I would have been off in another dream world. Admiring the new decor, I was thinking how my Nana would have loved to have a room like this back then. She always loved beautiful things. But, I have had enough remembering for one day. I am ready to retire for the night."

As they wandered down the stairs, Amanda wondered what room they had designated for her in the bungalow.

The bungalow, which had already been refurbished, had a lovely front porch with not much of a view just the rear of the big house. They went in the front door. The stairs to the second floor were just ahead of them. To the left were a large living room and an eat-in kitchen with lots of cupboards and a pantry. Amanda changed her mind about retiring so soon.

"It's a lovely evening so I think I will sit on the porch for a while and get some fresh air before I retire." Victoria stayed inside and joined Eddie and the kids watching TV and eating popcorn.

Rocking in what would become her favorite chair Amanda could not help but remember all the times she had sat on this porch with Boompa, Nana and Aunt Iris. There were so many memories…all the kids who became her friends that were guests in the big house during the season, while it was being run as a boarding house for the summer.

When she returned to the present moment, she discovered she was now ready for sleep.

The screen door slammed shut as she went inside, just as it had always done when she was a little girl. "Good night kids, I am going up to bed. Which room have you chosen for me?" "The second room on the right, as you go down the hall" Victoria replied. "We put your bags in there earlier. See you in morning."

Amanda readied herself for bed and climbed in tired and ready for sleep. She tossed and turned for a while as she remembered that this use to be her room during the summer season. Tired from the day's activities and her dreamtime fantasies she eventually drifted off into a good night's sleep.

The sun was steaming in the widow and woke her about 7:00 AM. She jumped in the shower, put on make-up and fixed her hair. She was ready for a new day. The smell of coffee brewing down in the kitchen and hearing the chatter of Catelyn and Scott sent her down the stairs quickly. She was still quite spry for a seventy year old.

"Good morning everyone", she announced as she came down the stairs.

Chapter 4

1873

After breakfast, I wandered back into the parlor and began starring at Jane's photograph once again. As I sat in one of the big old soft antique chairs, there seemed to be something hard under the cushion. I lifted the cushion and there in plain sight was a very old and tattered book. Surprised that no one had discovered it sooner, I picked it up and began reading it. I soon realized that it was Jane's journal. I knew that this was about to fill in some of the missing pieces of Jane's life and I was about to be enlightened...

It was not long before Jane began to notice that something unusual was happening to her body. At first, she ignored it and did not let on to Jonathan. Feeling that she most likely was pregnant, Jane knew that eventually she had to tell him. Fearful of her mother's reaction, she kept her secret for a time. However, her gut feeling was reinforced as an explosive argument ensued, when she finally disclosed the pregnancy to her mother. In an attempt to guard her reputation, she disregarded her mother's objection to a marriage. Jane and Jonathan were quickly united in holy wedlock at the local Protestant church in town. It was September of 1873, Jane was just 17, he was seven years older, and she was pregnant. Jane did all she could to conceal her pregnancy for a number of months, without success. When it became obvious, it was a perfect opportunity for the local gossipmongers. Less than nine months later a baby girl, Alice was born.

Alice Simpson, the first-born child of Jane and Jonathan, conceived out of wedlock, grew up knowing that her birth had caused a lot of talk on the island. Her school years were somewhat troublesome, but she was a great help to Jane during the difficult years that followed. Jane gave birth to a second child, a son William born two years later in August of 1876.

William was only six months old when the Simpson family moved from the village on the mainland to the island, in 1877. Due to the erratic nature of the fishing industry, Jonathan was in and out of work, so they struggled financially. They disagreed on many of the issues that help to keep marriages running smoothly. The household was not peaceful, and the children experienced the marital problems of their parents, during most of their early years.

Alice being a sensitive child involved herself in an imaginary dream world. When she entered school, she became a great reader, which provided her with an escape from the unhappy events that were taking place in her home. Jane worried about Alice always retreating into her books, absorbing herself in a make believe world and spending so much time alone. With a sweet personality and smile on her face, she was always willing to lend a hand if her mother needed it. Jane was grateful for that.

In spite of the troubled environment, William was a happy boy with an exceptionally good disposition and, he too, was always willing to please his mother. Up early in the morning he would jump out of bed, get his fishing pole and run down the hill to the shore. Watching the sunrise during his early morning trips to his favorite spot, he would fish until it was time for lunch. This was *his* respite from the unhappy moments he experienced at home. It made him feel safe and peaceful. A delightful child, whenever possible he was always at his mother's side, and she adored him.

Somehow, the children seemed to sense the turmoil Jane was experiencing about the marriage, and their father. Jonathan's erratic behavior unnerved the children so they both remained very close to their mother. Jane learned to focus on her children, which helped to keep her grounded. They provided her with the happier moments in her life.

Unfortunately, for Jane, her relationship with Jonathan was on a downward spiral. Early in the marriage, she learned very quickly that he was unreliable, abusive and controlling in their relationship. As she recalled their first encounter, it became so clear to her that this behavior should have been no surprise. She wondered why she had not seen it back then. Pondering some of their earlier encounters, she began to realize that her young age and innocence had something to do with it. Her marriage to Jonathan and the wisdom she gained as a result had changed all that. His control issues and her independent and self-sufficient attitude, created an extremely contentious atmosphere. They fought constantly over one thing or another. It drove him crazy that he could not get the best of her. She always stood up to him. However, most important for Jane, her primary focus became her determination to make a good life for her children.

Chapter 5

Corruption on the Island

Jonathan's reputation in the community had never been upstanding, but it was about to descend steadily into a much darker place. As the summer residents began to arrive, rumors circulated around the island that some of the new folks were of questionable character. The one person that had everyone gossiping was Jake Sparta. Introduced to Jonathan at a local pub, he immediately created a "beneficial" relationship when he learned about Jonathan's connections with the local sheriff's department. The rumors portrayed Jake as a big city con man who was involved in illegal activities. Jane's disapproval did not keep Jonathan from becoming involved. It was going to be an interesting summer season!

Weeks of inclement weather brought the fishing industry to a screeching halt. That meant Jonathan was not working or bringing in any income. Jane was constantly pressuring him and that was making him very irritable. Wanting to avoid Jane's constant badgering he began hanging out and drinking at the local pub with Jake. This association soon provided him with an opportunity for some very quick money, and questionable employment.

Jane was not privy to exactly what it was, but she knew she didn't like it and there seemed to be something crooked about it. He would disappear early in the morning and many times not even return in the evening. As usual, the island's rumor mill soon enlightened her that he was spending his evenings luring unsuspected folks off the street into an illegal card game at Jake's home. Using his ability to persuade people, he talked them into believing they could win lots of money. His powerful manipulation of these unsuspecting folks soon filled Jake's house, and was making Jonathan oodles of cash, although Jane would probably never see any of it. Conveniently for Jonathan and as a favor, the local sheriff looked the other way, even though he suspected illegal activity.

At the end of one evening when it came time for Jonathan to leave, one of the other players accused him of cheating and manipulating the winnings. There was a terrible argument that led to a fistfight between Jonathan and Jake. Jake's wife made an attempt to break up the fight but Jonathan swung at her knocking her to the floor where she lay bleeding. Both men were very drunk and a terrible situation followed. All the male spectators present seemed to be more interested in watching the two men trying to kill each other rather than attempting to stop the fight. Besides, they were fearful of interfering. Having an awareness of Jonathan's reputation and temper around the island, many of the locals avoided him whenever possible. It was not likely they would try to stop the fight, besides they were all drunk as well. In all the confusion, no one seemed to be concerned about the poor woman lying on the ground bleeding and almost unconscious. She laid there for what seemed like hours. When things quieted down and she was more, coherent she managed to get herself to a nearby house and the occupants drove her to the local hospital.

The next day it was reported in the local paper, "an ex-deputy named Jonathan Simpson struck a woman during a fight with Jake Sparta and left her laying on the ground bleeding." The incident became the talk of the town. On the mistaken idea that Jake's wife might die, the police arrested the two men. This would make Jonathan a murderer. When Jake's wife recovered and returned to her home a few days later, the police released both men. The local constable smoothed everything over by making a statement in the local paper. "Jonathan was drunk but is a decent chap and this would not have happened under different circumstances". Jonathan had many influential friends in important positions in town and got off scot-free. It always pays to have the local law enforcement agency in your corner. Even with his questionable reputation, he managed to escape any prosecution, because of the incident. Besides crimes against women being non-existent, women had no rights, and were second-class citizens. When it came to decisions made by the controlling male patriarchs of the day, women did not have any voice, and any laws protecting them from domestic violence were far off in the distant future.

Still out of work at the close of the season, Jonathan accepted his old job back as a deputy sheriff with the local police department. He knew he had to do something more to support his growing family and to keep his marriage from falling apart. His friends in high places in the local government always came in handy whenever he needed them. Corruption in law enforcement was quite common, and so they disregarded his troubled past. Nevertheless, trouble and his past were always lurking in the shadows.

Like a phantom in his own home he came and went as he pleased, so Jane was never quite sure where he was, or what he was doing. Shortly after the Jake Sparta incident, while working a late night shift on the mainland he had a terrible accident in an attempt to capture a local troublemaker. Running down a dark street chasing the perpetrator, he became the victim of a hit and run. The headline in the local paper the next day read, "Jonathan Simpson Fatally Wounded". Jane read the article without any feelings of grief concerning Jonathan. However, she began to worry how she would survive alone with her two children, and no husband. Fortunately, Jane had many loyal friends and neighbors in the community that were always there for her when she needed them, and so was her brother.

No other information became available as to Jonathan's condition. However, several weeks later, much to Jane's shock and surprise, he returned home. His behavior had become so unpredictable that she never knew what to expect. Having experienced a close encounter with the possibility of death unfortunately did not inspire Jonathan to live a better life nor did it transform him into a better husband or human being. He was back home again on a more regular basis, but nothing changed.

The household continued to be troubled. Determined and independent, Jane soon came to the realization that she could not depend on Jonathan for anything and began making her own plans. As gossip spread throughout the community, Jane made no bones about the fact that she was not happy with Jonathan or his erratic behavior. It was no secret either that he had been mean and abusive to her on numerous occasions. One night after a terrible argument, Jane insisted that he move out of the house for the sake of the children. He reluctantly complied and took a room at a local boarding house. However, Jonathan continued to come and go to their home as he pleased, and would show up at her door unexpectedly whenever he needed or wanted something. Jane was at her wits' end!

Anticipating that one day she might wind up alone with two children to support she decided to look for work to support her family. Not educated in an academic sense but very experienced in running a household Jane decided to look for work as a domestic at one of the local hotels or boarding houses. To her good fortune, she soon secured a position at The Oceanic Hotel. A new chapter in the life of Jane DuPris was about to begin but Jonathan and his antics were always hiding in the background, like a dark shadow in Jane's life.

Chapter 6
1883

I stopped reading the diary and came back to the present to learn that a couple of hours had passed. I wondered what everyone was doing and where the kids were. Actually quite surprised no one had come looking for me; I once again picked up the diary and began to drift back to into the story about Jane and her failing marriage. I thought, "What would the future hold for Jane?"...

Harold Camden

During the summer of 1883 while working a full schedule at the Oceanic Hotel Jane was finally introduced to the owner of the hotel, Harold Camden. He built, owned and operated hotels and boarding houses on the island and his friends knew him as "Harry". Harold Camden was a business leader and appeared to be a man totally unlike Jonathan Simpson. He had fought and maintained wounds from his participation in the Civil War, was a very well respected member of the community, a trustee on the board of a local bank, a volunteer with the local fire department and a participant in local Republican politics. At nineteen, he enlisted in the Army. His company engaged in many battles during the war. During one battle, he was injured and the source of that wound would give him trouble all during his life, and ultimately affect his overall health.

After meeting Jane, Harry soon learned through rumors in the community and newspaper articles, that she was married to an abusive man. Very attracted to her from their very first meeting, he had compassion for her and her unfortunate situation. Almost immediately, he began paying her a great deal of attention. As a kind and warmhearted man, he seemed to want to rescue her from this dreadfully, and at times horrific situation. Naturally, his behavior did not go unnoticed by the local busy-buddies. Still married to Jonathan she had to be careful, but the seeds of a new friendship were beginning to take root.

Jane, now 27 was still not a great beauty. Having been very much a homemaker, she dressed according to her station in life, in the simplistic fashion of the day. With her hair piled high upon her head, she usually went unnoticed by any men in her presence. However, Harry being a different kind of man noticed all the other finer qualities she possessed. He admired her independence, her wit, charm and most of all her work ethic so it was not long before they were having private conversations. He was several years her senior, extremely friendly and attentive, but always a "gentleman". Soon he began to hint at the possibility of calling on her. Even though he had just entered his forth decade, fortunately for Jane he was still single. As a successful entrepreneur, he had accumulated a great deal of financial and material success, as well as being a very prominent and well-respected businessperson, on the island.

"Stop and think, Jane!" she would scold herself, not wanting any additional problems in her life. She was tempted but tried hard to keep her distance and resist his attention. Nevertheless, he was persistent and very attracted to that self-sufficient attitude, which she always seemed to maintain. She, too, was attracted to him and very much enjoyed his attention; the kind she sought, but never received from Jonathan. She desperately tried always to remember that she still had a husband even though he was not living in the house any longer, and was never around.

Harry's curiosity but mostly his desire of her was gaining intensity. Before long, he was making deliberate attempts at pursuing her. She was very reluctant at first and tried to ignore his flirtations. Her defenses were beginning to crumble just as they had with Jonathan ten years earlier. More mature now she was very aware that she had to be more careful of her actions. Even so, around this small intimate community, the rumors spread, "Harry Camden has taken pity on this "very abused and mistreated woman". So once again, the happenings of her life were the cause of gossip. Contrary to her first relationship, this time it was about her close friendship with a wealthy and very prominent man in the business community. Much to her chagrin, events in her life continued to show up on the front page of the local newspapers. In addition, Jonathan was aware of the gossip. He was always somewhere hiding in the shadows taking it all in. Waiting for the perfect opportunity to make her the guilty party, he was planning to shout from the rooftops, about her inappropriate behavior.

Working full time, with two children at home, a house to take care of and an absentee husband every moment of Jane's life is full, with no time to spare. She really had limited opportunities for socializing and was very hesitant about getting involved in another relationship. She constantly must remind herself that she is still married to Jonathan, even though he is never around much to prove it, which she really does not mind at all. In fact, she is quite happy about it. It made her life a lot more peaceful. The children were also enjoying his absence, as well as the elimination of the continuous disturbing parental arguments, caused by his presence.

Harry had taken a fancy to her and was not about to give up. Working together on a daily basis gave them many opportunities to develop a strong bond between them and, of course, he had the ability to make it possible for the two of them to have some alone time together. After all, he owned the hotel and he was her immediate superior.

Several months later, and now completely absorbed with making more out of their friendship, Harry began making suggestions as to how they could spend some time alone away from the business activities of the day. Knowing she could not leave the children alone in the evening, Harry arranged for one of his trusted employees, Martha, to care for them while he and Jane had several very casual evenings out to themselves. They would go for a light dinner or for coffee and talk about the events of the day. He encouraged her ideas about operating the business and they talked about her children. All during these occasions, she was beginning to learn a great deal about the pros and cons of operating a hotel or boarding house business. A friendship and strong bond was beginning based on mutual admiration and respect, very much, in contrast to how her relationship with Jonathan had begun.

Harry, also intent on remembering that Jane was still a married woman tried to keep their friendship as respectable and secret as possible. Nevertheless, people living within small town mentality often busy themselves with gossip and talk about their neighbors. An intensely strong mutual attraction was beginning to grow and fortunately for Jane and Harry they chose not to let the town's rumor mill affect what was about to happen between them. Besides, Jane's behavior on most subjects never seemed to be dominated by the mores of the day. She was an independent thinking woman. She was not going to be told what to do or how to live her life by someone else's standards. It was not long before she was completely enjoying Harry's friendship and companionship. Jonathan was still staying out of sight.

With the passage of time as their friendship developed, they both seemed determined to continue no matter what people might have to say. It was probably the worse kept secret on the island. All their stolen moments became everyday gossip. Yes, at first it was just a friendship and Jane certainly needed a friend. However, during their private moments together what had been just a friendship was blossoming into something much deeper.

The season was over, business was now slowing down and it gave Harry the opportunity for more personal time. Jane remained cautious, and had her children to consider. Jonathan continued to be an absentee husband always off somewhere, and nowhere to be found.

After many months of casual evenings out together, Harry finally asked Jane for an official date. He wanted to take her to a very special place so they could have a night to themselves away from the scuttle-but in town. Jane accepted with delight and Harry arranged, once again, for one of his staff to take care of the children.

Being a romantic he made plans for them to take the ferry to the mainland, and then a carriage ride across state lines to a small town in New Hampshire with a charming secluded inn surrounded with mountains. It was a place Harry had been to many times for business meetings. He always felt that if he ever had anyone special in his life that he would take her there. Adjacent to the inn, overlooking a beautiful lake there was a quaint restaurant where Harry had previously made dinner reservations for the two of them. Here they felt an air of safety knowing they would not run into someone they knew.

The maitre d escorted them to a private table near the window with a view of the lake and mountains. Soft lighting in the room with gaslights, and candles on every table created a warm and inviting setting. In one corner, a fireplace burned brightly and added a lovely glow to the room. In the opposite one, there was baby grand piano where the piano player was tickling the ivories with soft romantic music. It was a perfect setting!

Cathy De Anne

After ordering dinner their conversation took on quite a different tone than they were accustomed to for business purposes. This evening was not going to include that type of idle chatter. Harry had things of great importance on his mind.

Jane needed to be upfront, and learned through unfortunate circumstances, that she had to be logical about her situation. Aware of that, she asked bluntly, with a big smile on her face, "Now that you have invited me out for a special evening and we are alone in this lovely place, I feel I must ask, "What intentions do you have in mind for us?"

With her past at the forefront of her mind, Jane had learned a very valuable lesson; she was a good deal wiser now. Cautious about making any rash decisions involving a man, and having been victimized by Jonathan, she was not about to step into the abyss that she had created with Jonathan.

Harry, taken aback for a moment, replied with a wink and a big smile on his face, "Only the best, I can assure you!" "I have had my eye on you for months now; I've watched how you work, how you have handled your unfortunate situation at home and how you care for your children. You have taken charge of your life, without a husband you can depend on, and I admire and respect that."

Continuing he said, "On another note my fondness for you is no secret! I believe that this feeling has become mutual. I hope that I am right in assuming that."

Listening intently to his words Jane took a few moments before responding. "Yes, you are correct I am fond of you and I value and appreciate you, your friendship and all the kindnesses you have shown me."

Jane, "I want to be as upfront with you as you have been with me. The truth is that I am falling in love with you and I would like our friendship to become much more than just a friendship, I hope you are aware of that." "Yes, Harry, I have sensed that, and I am quite pleased about it." Jane, still not tipping her hand completely about her own feelings was choosing her words carefully. "Since I am still married I feel I must tread lightly about getting romantically involved with another man, but yes I have become more than fond of you. You might assume that I, too, am falling in love. The question becomes what are we going to do about this?"

With that, dinner arrived and interrupted their conversation. Always with the right words at the right time Harry said, "We will continue talking about this at another time but for now let's enjoy the present moment, the ambiance of this wonderful place, and the food."

At the conclusion of dinner, they left and returned to the carriage that was waiting to take them to the ferry. Before Jane had a chance to step into the carriage Harry took her hand, put his free hand around her waist and pulled her toward him. They looked intensely into each other's eyes and he kissed her passionately. Then he released his grip on her and allowed her to turn and climb into the carriage. Just before she did she looked into his eyes once more and smiled lovingly at him. He instantly knew that she was pleased about the entire evening. This would be their special place whenever they could steal some time alone. Like a knight in shining armor, Harry was intent on rescuing her. This was the first of many trips to the Green Lantern Inn and Restaurant.

As the carriage pulled up in front of her house, he got out and escorted her to her front door. She thanked him for a lovely evening. He said nothing but very gently kissed her on the cheek and said good night. In a moment he was gone and out of sight.

As she turned to go through the door, she heard some rustling in the bushes. Suddenly, Jonathan was in her face. "Just what do you think you are doing? You seem to have forgotten that you are still my wife!"

Jane retorted, "No, I have not forgotten, but you are never around and you do not contribute in any way to this household. So, I really don't think about you at all!" I thought you had left town, so if you have not, please just go away and leave me alone. Why do not you find a lawyer and file for divorce? That would be the best thing that could happen for both of us."

Filled with anger, Jonathan yelled in her face, "Oh no, you are not going to get off that easy. You will start behaving or I will not be responsible for the consequences."

"Don't you threaten me, Jonathan Simpson," Jane demanded.

Hearing all the loud conversation outside the babysitter opened the door. Jonathan became startled, and turned and ran into the woods. Jane felt rescued from a disturbing confrontation. She suspected this would not be the last one.

As Jane went inside, she knew she had to calm her nerves from her encounter with Jonathan. Martha, the babysitter offered to make her a cup of tea and she accepted. She had become acquainted with Martha through work. She was a kind and devoted employee to Harry and he trusted her implicitly. When the tea was ready, they sat and chatted. By the time Martha left, Jane had regained her composure.

As she lay in bed thinking about the evening, she put the incident with Jonathan aside and thought about her time with Harry. He was kind and loving and he wanted to take care of her and her children, she knew that. Overwhelmed with joy about their discussion and the entire evening she just smiled to herself.

Suddenly, thoughts of Jonathan wandered back into her mind. They were disturbing but she wanted to relish in the moments of her time with Harry. She did not feel much like sleeping that night and remembered another evening a long time ago after her first date with Jonathan. Thankfully, this time it was different. Harry was honorable and a respected member of the business community. Experience is a great teacher and Jane had grown up and learned a great lesson.

While Jane and Harry's friendship was blossoming, Jonathan, now living alone, was secretly making plans of his own. After his recent encounter with Jane, he was more determined than ever. The rumors had not escaped his ears. Having a bruised ego and feeling humiliated on a daily basis, their relationship was still making scandalous front-page news in the local newspaper.

Chapter 7

Secrets and Scandal

I came back to the present momentarily to realize all was still quiet and no one seemed to be looking for me. They all must be busy, so I continued to read as I drifted back into the story of Jane and Harry...

Not working and with idle time on his hands as a result of his accident, Jonathan soon began to be obsessed with suspicions about his wife and her relationship with Harold Camden. The gossip was everywhere and even one overzealous and very sleazy reporter wrote a sarcastic article in the local paper. When Jonathan read it, his temperamental and impulsive imagination went into high gear, and presented him with all kinds of sordid mental pictures of his wife with another man.

Angry and jealous he said to himself, "How can she do this to me? The entire town is talking about this and she is making me look like a fool." The situation drove him crazy. He began conjuring up and planning various ways to catch the two of them and accuse them of being lovers. "This must stop or I'll show them!"

Strolling through town one day, a reporter from the local paper stopped Jonathan and asked him, "What do you think about your wife's relationship with Harold Camden?" He did not need very much prompting to get him to talk about the subject that the entire town was whispering about. Just the asking of the question made him so angry that the veins in his neck looked like they were going to burst.

"I'll tell you what I think…their so-called friendship is making me look like the laughing stock in this community. Her relationship with Harold Camden, owner of the hotel where she is employed is of an illicit nature. I can no longer put up with it and I am leaving town."

Some weeks passed and the same paper ran another article confirming that he had gone away due to the scandal that was taking place regarding his wife and her "Harry". Nevertheless, Jonathan was laying low and attempting to maintain some self-control. He was not going anywhere but biding his time waiting for the right opportunity to set a trap and confront the two lovers. As the situation kept eating away at him, Jane and Harry's relationship was getting better all the time.

An orchestra from New York City arrived on the island to do a concert of Puccini music and Harry bought tickets for him and Jane. While waiting in the lobby for the concert to begin Jane over-heard some folks saying that Jonathan was back in town, again. Jane looked at Harry and blurted out, "I knew he was up to something. Pretending to leave was just a scheme. I know how manipulative he is and I am sure he remained in town but just stayed out of sight. He is biding his time waiting for things cool down in order to make his next move".

One evening while Jane was working, Jonathan managed to obtain access to his home where he had resided with Jane. Encountering the children, who were being cared for, once again by Martha, his mind immediately became devious. He began questioning her and the children continuously about Jane's activities, especially concerning Mr. Camden. Martha politely asked him to leave, but he paid no attention to her and continued questioning the children. The kids, of course, being young were ready to tell all to their father. Learning that Harry would sometimes come to call at a certain time in the evening, he began to make his plans for a confrontation.

A week later Jane was running late on her way home from work to meet Harry at the house. The children were staying at Martha's home for the evening. Jonathan, up to no good, began sneaking around their house. Still having a key he let himself in and sat in the parlor waiting and hoping that Harry would arrive. When the doorbell rang, he went to the door and opened it. Grinning, in his normal cocky way, he just stood with the door ajar for a few silent moments, just glaring at Harry. Harry, expecting to see Jane, was stunned when Jonathan opened the door. Sarcastically, retaining the grin on his face, Jonathan invited him in and blurted out, "Surprised to see me?"

Harry was wise to him and remained composed. Not wishing to cause a scene he immediately turned on his heel, stepped off the porch and disappeared as quickly as his legs could carry him, leaving Jonathan standing there with his mouth hanging open. Harry was not anxious to have a confrontation with Jonathan in lieu of the scandal that was keeping the town's gossip mill alive and well. But, Jonathan was intent on confronting his wife's lover, and was frustrated since Harry had disappeared so quickly. Jonathan was not going to leave this alone.

Later that evening Jonathan paid a visit to Harry at the hotel. Standing behind the reception desk Harry saw him coming. With a scowl on his face, Jonathan approached the desk and demanded, "Harold Camden, you are never to, so much, as look at Mrs. Simpson again." He hoped that this threat would intimidate Harry into discontinuing his association with Jane. Nevertheless, quite the opposite occurred when Harry politely told him "If you threaten me again I shall have you arrested." Jonathan knew that Harry was a very powerful member in the community. Cowardice was beneath the surface of Jonathan's personality, and the fear he felt inwardly made him back down. He left the hotel but returned to the house and waited for Jane to come home so that he could confront her. He speculated that if he could not intimidate Harry, he seemed sure he could intimidate Jane. He was not giving up.

The next evening while at home waiting for Harry, Jane had just finished dressing when a knock came to the door. She expected it to be the kids and Martha. Much to her surprise, when she opened the door she encountered Jonathan. "What are you doing here?" she said with disdain.

"I'll tell you what I am doing here…I have had enough of this talk about you and your so-called friend, Harry." "I want it stopped immediately!" he demanded.

The veins in his neck were bulging again he was so angry. Jane being very self-assured ordered him to leave which made him even angrier. He had all he could do to keep from striking her. She considered threatening him with calling the police but she was well aware that he knew all the local law enforcement officials, and they would most likely take his side. She was very forceful in her determination to have him leave and tactfully pleaded with him, "The children are on their way home I don't want them exposed to anything that would upset them so please leave now for their sake." Mentioning the children seemed to hit a more sensitive nerve. No matter what, he did love his kids and so he backed off. Knowing Jonathan, Jane presumed it was not going to stop there.

The next day the scandal actually showed up in the local newspaper and once again, Jane's life became the talk of the island. Jonathan left town again and stayed out of sight for a number of weeks until the gossip subsided.

When Jonathan finally returned he went directly to the local paper to set the record straight. He demanded that they print an article stating that he was accusing Harold Camden of having improper relations with his wife. Harry in response denied the charge and denounced Jonathan as an abusive husband and a loafer.

Jonathan was beginning to feel like he was losing the battle until he met his wife at a local restaurant where she was waiting to meet Harry. "This is my opportunity," he thought.

It had been more than a month since their confrontation at the house. By this time he was obsessed at trying to make one last attempt at controlling her. As he approached her she tried desperately to ignore him. They had a fierce quarrel and she demanded emphatically that he stay away from her. She politely told him that Harry was a true gentleman, a man of integrity and she and the children would be taken care of. Desperately attempting to get back in her good graces he suddenly moved closer to her and tried to hug her. Her strong independent nature reared its ugly head with a slap across his face, and she vehemently spurned his attentions. His ego bruised in front of all the people who were witnessing their encounter, he briskly walked away. Trying to compose himself and deciding what to do, Jonathan moved out of sight. His insides were boiling like a kettle of hot soup.

Later as Jane was leaving the building he once again attempted to restrain her and this time when she resisted he assaulted her and knocked her to the floor. The manager of the restaurant immediately came to her rescue and instructed one of the waiters to escort him out of the building. With his temper totally out of control, he came face to face with Harry outside the restaurant, who was hurrying to meet Jane. He assaulted him with violent blow to the head, knocking him down a flight of stairs, and then fled. During the fall Harry dislocated his ankle. After that incident, Jonathan disappeared. The next morning Harry procured a warrant for his arrest. Later that week, found, arrested and arraigned at a local court, Jonathan receives a suspended sentence.

The next day the local paper ran an article quoting Jane, "My husband Jonathan Simpson is a loafer and abusive. His accusations regarding Mr. Camden and myself are the result of his controlling and jealous nature.

I have supported him and his two children for the last couple of years and I am quite tired of his behavior. Mr. Camden has been a kind friend and I do not appreciate the scandalous stories he has circulated about the two of us. He has abandoned me and his children, and I shall never live with him again!"

It was now 1884 and with that statement, the Simpson marriage finally ended. Jonathan disappeared and Jane never heard directly from him again.

However, there was no divorce!

Chapter 8

2010

A summer shower with lots of lightning and thunder brought me back to reality. A good part of the day had passed. Actually, I now wondered why no one was looking for me. Just as I finished that thought, I heard footsteps thumping up the porch stairs like a herd of elephants. "Nana, Nana" they yelled, "Where are you?" "We're coming to find you." As they entered the parlor, they were giggling, almost as if they were up to something. "Mommy is looking for you." "OK," I'm coming...."

"Mom, where have you been all afternoon?" "Just nosing around," Amanda replied.

"Eddie and I have been so busy in the store organizing things and beginning to get ready for our first guests who arrive next week that we completely forgot about you."

Amanda snapped back, "Oh, you don't have to concern yourselves about me. I know how to fill my time. You two need to continue to do the things you need to do. However, you can let me know when and if I can help at all. I will be happy to do so"

"Thanks, Mom."

"As a matter of fact, how would you like me to prepare the dinner tonight?" Amanda asked.

"That would be wonderful. Then we could finish up what we are working on."

"Consider it done," Amanda replied.

Amanda prepared an scrumptious dinner enjoyed by all. Victoria, Eddie and the kids cleared the table and did all the dishes.

"Let's all take a walk down to the ocean and watch the sunset," Amanda suggested and everyone agreed.

As they all descended the hill to the shoreline, they noticed that the ocean was unusually calm. The sun was just beginning to set and streams of light rays were glistening on the water. Bright blue sky and billowy white clouds began to turn somewhat pink as the sun moved toward the horizon.

"This is such a spectacular location and one of the main reasons why we had to have this house; besides the fact that it had once belonged to our family. "I heartily approve." said Amanda.

The house's location on the western side of the island, and with no obstruction, made the sun appear to slide down into the water. Amanda, Victoria and Eddie relished in the beauty of the moment while the children played at the shore.

"OK, kids, it's time to go back up to the house, let's go!" Victoria commanded.

The next morning Amanda awakened fresh and ready for another beautiful day.

Chapter 9

Jane and Harry

With breakfast concluded, I headed back to the Cottage. Obsessed with Jane's life story, I wanted to find out what happened next. In the parlor next to Jane's photograph was one of her beloved Harry that we had found in the attic. I continued to read and learned some of what I already knew, and lots more from her diary...

Jane and Harry's courtship was now in full bloom. They have made several trips to their favorite place, the Green Lantern Inn. Then one evening while there having dinner, Harry asked if Jane would consider living with him. They both knew they could not marry since she was still married to Jonathan. She was reluctant but Jane was now very much in-love and wanted more than anything to share her life with him.

"Harry, before we take any steps in that direction we need to talk to my children." As time went on they had also grown to love Harry so Jane knew that there would be a problem. The next evening they presented the children with their plan. The kids adored Harry and the decision received approval. They moved into a large house on the island owned by Harry.

Harry was a kind and gentle companion and he did take care of her and her two children, as she knew he would. He became the father they never really had and the children grew to love him and had a wonderful relationship with him. As the children matured into adults, Jane and Harry's relationship thrived and they lived together for many years without the benefit of marriage. Still married to another man, this type of living arrangement was most unacceptable at the time. There were only two grounds for divorce at the time, abandonment or adultery. Due to the arcaic laws of the day women did not have permission to file suit for divorce and, unfortunately, had no rights on these issues. Jonathan's absence regarding the abandonment issue and Jane's infidelity, kept the idea of divorce in the shadows and out of reach.

The community was well aware that Jonathan had been an unsuitable, abusive husband so the rumor mill remained at an all-time low. Friends, neighbors and even the local newspaper seemed to ignore the couple's living situation and left them alone. Harry was highly regarded in the community as was Jane's brother, who by this time had become a very successful banker. Their reputations and standing in the community were enough to keep any unfavorable or scandalous chatter from getting out of hand, and the gossipmongers remained quiet.

Some months later, one evening sitting in the parlor after a long days work, Harry quietly approached Jane and asked her to marry him. She, of course was still married to Jonathan so they were not sure how they would handle that situation. After a much discussion, they decided to put it on hold. Harry continued to thrive in business and Jane was always there to support anything he did. They often wondered what Jonathan was up to, and what nonsense what happening in his life.

Chapter 10

Where is Jonathan?

According to what I had learned from Victoria's research, Jonathan's life was always turning up in the newspaper. That was nothing new for him. It was that avenue of information, which kept Jane informed, as to his whereabouts and shenanigans.

Knowing that nothing was resolved, due to his arrest for assaulting Harry, Jane heard via the grapevine that he continued to work as a police officer until about 1886. However, Jonathan did not completely disappear. She learned of his whereabouts mostly through newspaper articles since he never returned to the island. He was always up to something, and whatever it was, always seemed to make the local headlines.

First news of Jonathan appears in the local island paper in August of 1890. He has now honored himself with the title of Jonathan Simpson, Boat Captain. This seemed like a natural choice since he has descended from a long line of seafarers on both sides of his family. The article reveals that as captain of a large charter yacht he runs aground. During the incident, a fire breaks out from a grease spill. Jonathan and the rest of the crew escape with their lives, but the fire destroys the yacht. The paper calls him a hero for rescuing all the passengers. Once again, he escapes any ill-fated future. Sometime after that incident, he accepted a job working at a yacht club on the mainland, close to where he maintained a residence. The article also states that he met and married a young woman half his age, even though he has never bothered to divorce Jane. Mumbling, as she concludes reading, "Nothing about Jonathan's behavior ever surprises me."

Chapter 11

Jane & Harry 1892 - 1896

I came back to the present for a moment, and then continued to read the next episode in Jane and Harry's life...

A few pleasant and uneventful years passed and once again, Jane and Harry discussed the idea that they might marry. They had no children of their own but Harry was a wonderful stepfather to Jane's two children.

Alice, now a mature young woman meets a young man, named Richard Langley who was visiting the island from New York with his parents. It was not long before there was a romantic attraction and the two became inseparable. They were married after a short courtship and made their permanent home in New York. Within a year, Alice gave birth to a son. Due to her profound fondness for Harry, she named the child Harold Camden Langley for her stepfather. Harry had become the man in Alice's life who was more of a father to her than her own had been. She and her family enjoyed their life in New York. In order to spend some time with Jane, they returned to the island for an extended stay, during the season with their young son.

Jane's son William, who was only ten when Jane left Jonathan, thrived through the years in Harry's household and grew to honor, and deeply respected his stepfather. Despite the unfortunate atmosphere early in the home, William grew into a fine young man. He became a firefighter in the local fire department. After several years, forced to leave on a disability due to smoke inhalation, he took up carpentry, and later worked for the railroad. As an active and productive member of the island community, and well known, in his own right. Always devoted to his mother William remained at home until such time that he might marry.

Unfortunately, Jane and Harry's plans to marry had to remain on hold. In 1892 a great fire destroyed many, many buildings on the island. Harry suffered some losses along with many of the properties that were lost. Thankfully, no one perished but Harry's buildings were underinsured and he lost a great deal of money. Nevertheless, he found a way to rebuild the old structures and add one or two new ones during the next several months. The one structure he put his whole heart and soul into was a lovely Victorian boarding house that he named "the DuPris Cottage" in honor of his beloved Jane. Once completed, he sold it to a local businessperson. Harry really did not want to sell it but they needed the money. As part of the sale, he negotiated for Jane to manage it during the season. She then employed several people to help her run it. She was able to bring in some additional income for them, but, Harry's finances were hard hit and they struggled.

Later that same year Harry decided to retire from the building business but remained proprietor of the hotel where he and Jane had met. Now in his fiftieth year his health was beginning to fail, due to the old war injury to his leg.

Unmarried and living together for many years Jane and Harry decided that enough time had now passed and they were determined that they should marry. Besides, there was another reason now. Still of childbearing age, Jane had just announced to Harry that she was pregnant. They were both surprised but overjoyed at the idea that there would be a child, because of their union. However, knowing that she was still legally married to Jonathan, they were well aware that they had to avoid any charges of bigamy and another child conceived out of wedlock. Of course, Jonathan was nowhere to be found, and had not been heard from in almost ten years. Therefore, they left Maine and crossed the state line into New Hampshire. There they went to a Justice of the Peace. Jane declared herself single, used her maiden name and they were married. For their first night as husband and wife, they returned to their favorite place, The Green Lantern Inn where their romance had first become official. It was the spring of 1896.

Chapter 12

Unexpected New Life

The first year of their marriage seemed to fly by. There was great joy especially over the fact that a new life was stirring inside of Jane. Harry was thrilled at the idea of having a child of his own, this late in his life with Jane, who had just turned forty-one.

One snowy morning early in February of 1897, Jane woke Harry announcing that her labor was beginning. He got up and made them both coffee, and called the doctor.

Late that afternoon after several hours of hard labor, a beautiful baby boy came into their lives. Thomas Camden was christened a month later at the local church that was so much a part of Jane's life. Even with all the gossip that had surrounded them through the years, their close friends were just thrilled for this new happiness they were about to experience.

Thomas was an adorable happy child. He was their "love child" and became the center of their life, since the other children were grown. Alice was married, but William remained part of their household. He adored little Tommy and was a great help to his mother and Harry.

Chapter 13

Joys and Shadows

Tommy's first birthday was rapidly approaching and the family was beginning to arrive. William, still employed and traveling with the railroad, would be sure to be present for the celebration. Jane's daughter Alice was coming with her family. There was a lot of excitement and anticipation surrounding this joyful event. A beautiful cake and a mountain of presents covered table.

During all the festivities, the joy quickly diminished when Alice suddenly became quite ill. Alice's illness lasted for several weeks with the anticipation of a full recovery. When typhoid fever set in, she took a turn for the worse. It was only a matter of days when she unexpectedly passed away of complications due to pneumonia, leaving her husband alone, and her young son without a mother. Devastated, Jane experienced a great sense of loss and emptiness in her heart that followed her through the years, and never seemed to vanish.

After the funeral, and with the summer season ending, Alice's husband Richard, now a young widower took his young son and returned to New York. Young Harold, or

Junior as everyone came to call him, was only six at the time. The death of his mother left him with feelings he did not understand. They had been so close, and without her, he cried himself to sleep every night. His father also felt very alone and did not seem to be able to comfort him. As Richard struggled to care for his young son, he continually searched for a new wife, one who could be a stepmother to his son.

Before long, while visiting a relative in the city he met a newly widowed woman. She had no children of her own. Thinking it a perfect situation, he courted and married her within the year. They seemed to be happy, but young Harold, missed his mother and with time grew more melancholy. As he grew into a young man, he was not fond of his new stepmother. Unhappy and restless as he entered his teenage years Junior grew to intensely dislike his stepmother. He was not sure what he was going to do about it, but knew his life had to change.

Chapter 14

Tommy

Jane found solace during this time of grief about Alice by focusing on Tommy, and the great joy that continued to fill her heart from this wonderful little boy. He was a sweet child with big brown eyes and dirty blond hair. He looked a lot like Jane. Active and curious it was becoming harder for Jane to keep up with him as she was still managing the DuPris Cottage.

Coming as a shock to Jane, rumors were floating around town that Jonathan had shown his face again and was looking for her. What could he possibly want from her after all this time? Actually, she remembered that nothing he ever did really surprised her, but she was anxious about it.

Two weeks later, he showed up at the DuPris Cottage. It was a quiet afternoon and her work was pretty much finished, for the day. Tommy was playing with some toys in the foyer, when the door burst open, and she heard someone calling her name. She could not mistake the sound of that voice calling her every name possible. He had been at the local pub. Some busy-buddy had told him about Tommy and that she and Harry were married. He was in a rage and very drunk. Of course, he knew that there had never been any divorce. He staggered over to her and grabbed her arm pulling her toward the door while repeating obscenities about her. She tried to get free of him without success. He continued to pull her out the door down the street, and into a carriage. As he did, Tommy got up and ran after her calling, Mommy, Mommy. Jonathan whipped the horse and he started to gallop. Tommy ran out into the street just as the carriage sped by. Caught up in horse's legs and the wheels of the carriage, his little body trampled. Jonathan whipped the horse repeatedly, still calling Jane all kinds of names. She was screaming as she helplessly watched the horror that unfolded in front of her eyes.

Adrenaline, rushing through her body, she regained some strength, pushed Jonathan off his seat and he fell out of the carriage. She was able to bring the horse to a standstill. Hysterical, she jumped out of the carriage and ran to Tommy who was lying lifeless in the street. Several folks had already gathered around him. Her brother, hearing the commotion in the street left his desk in the bank to see what was going on. When he saw her coming, he grabbed her and put his arms around her, saying there is nothing you can do for him now. Jane, hysterical and sobbing uncontrollably, he was not able to comfort her. An ambulance showed up and took Tommy to the hospital. Harry, across town at a construction site, received word of the accident.

A short time later, they all met at the hospital. Harry and Jane both devastated and in shock, could not be consoled. Jane's brother wondered to himself how they would ever survive this tragedy.

The local sheriff declared the incident a tragic accident and put Jonathan in a cell to sleep off his drunken stupor. Both Jane and Harry knew that Jonathan was responsible which did not seem to matter to the police.

Of course, the story made the front page of the local paper. Once again, their lives became center stage for the local rumor mill. They found strength in each other, in their community, and in their work. They were changed and saddened, but they went on without the joy and the love of their precious little boy. In quiet moments, Jane would sometimes wonder if this terrible tragedy was her penance for not following the rules of her society. However, she would quickly dismiss those thoughts as ridiculous, since she deeply believed in her heart in the goodness and forgiveness of the creator. She had come to know that there are no accidents and that there is a reason for everything. Lessons, whether joyful or sorrowful, are a part of everyone's journey. All through life, she had a loving, generous heart and remained a tower of strength, no matter what the circumstances.

Chapter 15

2010

"Mom, are you back in the parlor again, daydreaming about Jane?" Somewhat groggy and with tears in her eyes, Amanda answered, "Yes, I am." "So what have you come up with, besides what we already know? "Oh, really nothing just the romantic notions of an older lady attempting to put herself in Jane's shoes." "Well Mom, come back to reality and let's go into town for a little shopping spree for dinner. I feel like having some fresh lobster...how about you?"

Amanda and Victoria got on their bikes, equipped with baskets and went into town. They wandered the streets, looked in the shop windows and exchanged greetings with some of the town's folks. Beginning to get hungry, their stomachs directed the next stop at the fish market, where the boats brought in fresh lobster daily.

Lobster tails and claws dipped in drawn butter, with baked potatoes and broccoli made everyone lick their lips with joy as they finished dinner. Amanda bought fresh made ice cream and that completed the meal...especially for the kids.

Following an hour or so of complete relaxation, it was time to retire for the night. The days till the grand opening and their first guests were not far away, but there was still work to be completed. Everyone went his or her separate ways looking forward to a restful night's sleep.

Amanda opened her window wide to let in the fresh sea air. It was heavenly! She slept like a baby.

Chapter 16

Harry & Jane's Golden Years

As dawn arrived, I promptly got up, dressed in something comfortable, grabbed a blanket and went down to the beach. I arrived just in time to see the light of the sun beginning to come up over the horizon. It was a spectacular morning, crisp and cool and the ocean was like a sea of glass. I spread the blanket and plopped myself down and continued to read Jane's diary. As I did, I chuckled to myself, "I hope I can get up when it's time to leave!"

As I sat there enjoying the beauty of nature and the sun moving up in the sky my thoughts returned to Jane. This might have been where she first made love to Jonathan. If that were true, it was no wonder she fell in love with him at that moment. Now, the years had changed all that, and she was growing older with Harry....

During the years that followed, Harry suffered some very significant business losses and the stress was taking its toll on his health. The injury from the war continued to contribute to many of his health problems. Not able to work and earn a living any longer, he was now collecting a meager pension from the government, because of his years of service in the army during the Civil War. Jane continued to help at the hotel and manage the DuPris Cottage. All her chores were now more of an effort as she too was getting older, and Harry was not around to help. She persevered and strived with resolve and no thought of surrendering to any difficulty. William was a huge asset and helped as much as he could, but he had a full time job, so his time was limited.

When Harry became too ill to live at home, he decided to enter a government run facility for retired army personnel, which was quite a distance from their home. After much discussion, they both agreed that this was the best solution and they prepared for the trip. There he lived away from his beloved Jane, and his absence devastated her. She made several train trips to spend time with him. The army facility was a long way to travel from the island and she still had to maintain the business for the income it provided her. She longed for him to be back home where she could care for him. Working full time and with a home to care for would not leave her much spare time to care for Harry. In the end, circumstances forced them both to accept the fact that he would stay at the center where he would be well cared for by the nurses. This would relieve her of any undue burden. Entering her senior years, she just did not have the same stamina or energy that she once possessed. With Harry no longer at her side to support her, loneliness consumed much of her day.

Over the next few years, when time permitted, she spent a lot of time making train trips to visit him. Then one day she received a telegram that he was going downhill quickly and she should come at once. Many of his health issues had exacerbated since he had first entered the facility.

The DuPris Cottage, totally booked during August, Jane wondered how she would get time off. Somehow, she was able to get a replacement for her work. William took some time off from his job and oversaw the management of the Cottage. All her responsibilities now covered she made plans to go and stay with Harry for a few days.

Seeing her enter his room, he was ecstatic and tears of joy were welling up in his eyes, especially learning she was to spend several days. They hugged each other intensely for a long time. Hours upon hours passed as she sat along side his bed talking, reading to him and feeding him. Instead of going back to her hotel in the evening, she would sit in a chair next to the bed and fall asleep, always holding his hand. Almost a week passed and one night, about three in the morning a strange noise startled her. As she awakened and became more conscious of her surroundings, she immediately sensed that his hand was ice cold, and she could no longer hear his labored breathing. She suddenly screamed for the nurse, although she already knew what the nurse was going to tell her. Tears were rolling down her cheeks now, and she began to sob.

Another great emptiness found its way into her heart when on that night in August 1903 at the age fifty-eight Harry had peacefully passed away in his sleep. She felt so comforted that she had made the trip to be with him during his last days. Truly saddened by this loss and grieving, Jane's finances are now non-existent, except for her meager income at the Cottage. All of Harry's assets that would have passed on to her were depleted by his hospitalization.

Funeral arrangements are already in place, as Harry's remains arrive back on the island. Filled to capacity, the memorial service was at the local church. In attendance were friends, relatives and many local business people. Harry had been a pillar of the community and they all came to honor him. His body laid to rest in the adjacent churchyard.

After a short grieving period, Jane attempted to get a government pension as Harry's widow. That continued for several years to no avail. The fact that she had never been divorced from Jonathan and not considered Harry's legal widow, the pension denied. Social Security was still decades away.

At a time when women were still so dependent on men for support, she might have succumbed to another fate, but not Jane. Built for her by Harry, the DuPris Cottage was going to be hers, and all the months and months she had managed it, she was determined to buy it. Not exactly sure how she would accomplish it but one day she believed in her heart it was going to be hers. With the help of her brother at the bank, and her knowledge of inn keeping, this self-sufficient, strong-willed woman was eventually able to secure a mortgage and buy the lovely Victorian boarding house on Seagull Beach Drive, which Harry had dedicated to her.

During 1904 and over the next few years she worked hard, received many guests and ran it successfully with the help of her son William. He took care of the things she was not able to do herself. At the same time employed by the railroad and working both places, he was busy all the time. Using the skills and the experiences Jane had gained during her years working with Harry, she eventually returned to financial stability. An achievement not often realized by a single woman during the early 1900's.

Jane was a true survivor and although she missed Harry terribly and grieved for a number of months, she was not about to let widowhood keep her down. As a businessperson, she became a very active member of the community and was a long-standing member of the church where she had married Jonathan. Following in Harry's example, she became involved in some of the local politics and the Eastern Star, a feminine counterpart of the Masons.

Early one morning in August 1907, while reading the local paper Jane learns as she read a headline…"Jonathan Simpson, Dead at 58!" Continuing to read the obituary, she learned that Jonathan has passed away of a stroke. Calling out to William, she handed him the newspaper. Learning of his father's death William, somewhat saddened, decided to attend the funeral out of respect. Jane, for reasons of her own, decided not to attend.

William continued to live on with his mother and remained her only support. With both husbands now deceased, Jane was officially a widow. Her son William, still single, became her close companion and confidant assisting her in running the boarding house, and handling all her financial affairs. As 1910 approached, Jane had been contentedly operating a very successful boarding house with several boarders and one domestic employee, to help her with all the housekeeping and cooking chores.

Nevertheless, fate has other plans for Jane when she feels obligated to admit a new member to her household. Without any warning, her teenage grandson Junior arrived at the DuPris Cottage and announced to Jane that he wants to live with her, and has claimed her as his adopted mother. At the same time, he dropped his birth name of Langley and began to call himself Harold Camden, Junior. This new addition to the household will create future years of unrest for the entire family, and for some not yet part of the household.

Chapter 17

Junior

While wandering around the cottage I entered the family dining room. A good amount of family discussions took place here around the dinner table. When I was about 9 years old, I remember listening carefully to a very intense argument over my grandfather's will. One name kept coming up, Junior....

His teenage years behind him, Junior eventually left his grandmother's home and started out on his own. He remained estranged from his father and stepmother. He was immature and constantly floundered during his young years. Always troubled with his life in turmoil, and with nowhere to turn, he continuously landed on his grandmother's doorstep.

Feeling sorry for him, she always found some way to help him, and usually allowed him to re-join the household. Very aware of Junior's antagonistic behavior toward the family and boarding house guests, she refused him living space in the main house. This time things were going to be different. The bungalow in the rear of the DuPris Cottage was currently vacant and she suggested that he move in there and pay her a small amount of monthly rent. Having no other option, he agreed.

While living separately from the rest of the family he still violated certain boundaries and maintained an outrageous lack of respect. His feelings of entitlement and his comings and goings from the main house whenever it suited his fancy, kept the family constantly irritated. Having a soft spot in her heart, Jane was much too tolerant of Junior's behavior. With respect and some attempt at diplomacy, William pleaded with his mother to address the situation.

Difficult and demanding from the very beginning Junior, with a rude sense of privilege, continuously argued and upset his grandmother. Trying to protect his Mom William got involved, and that always resulted in more tension and arguments for all concerned. In 1913, Junior met and married a very young local woman against his grandmother's advice. A few weeks into the marriage, they had several brutal quarrels. At the urging of his grandmother, and with the promise of a car and the possibility of a house in the future, he agreed to divorce her. He received the car immediately but only half of a house in her will. He settled for the decision but was not happy about it. Anger and frustration about not getting his own way put him on a path that would create a dark shadow in the lives of Jane and her descendants, for years to come.

Chapter 18

William's Marriage to Mary Mitchell

My grandfather, William or Boompa, as I named him as a toddler and we all called him, was a wonderful father and grandfather. I have been a good part of his life and have so many loving memories of him...

Employed with the railroad, gave William many opportunities to travel. In 1910 during the summer season, while visiting the wine country in Vermont, he toured a beautiful vineyard. William had matured into a very good-looking young man. Appearing quite handsome and sophisticated, there he noticed Mary Mitchell, the daughter of the local mayor. Outfitted in a gorgeous hat and a blue silk dress to match she was stunning and well dressed. Immediately attracted, his eyes remained focused on her. Following the tour, during the wine tasting he approached her and introduced himself. She was polite and responsive but what he did not know was that she was to be the entertainment for the afternoon, along with her sister Iris. Mary was an accomplished pianist and her sister was a singer, who had toured the US with a well-known opera company for several years, against her parent's wishes.

After the performance, William wandered over to where they were standing. Many guests had gathered around them with compliments. As the guests moved away, he deliberately walked up to them and introduced himself. He complimented both Mary and her sister on their performance, and asked if they might consider being his guest at the local pastry shop for tea. Mary was immediately attracted to him but was somewhat hesitant. She very much wanted to accept but he was a stranger. She glanced at her sister who winked with approval. Then just at that very moment, she glanced across the room and noticed her father starring at them with a curious look on his face.

"Thank you for your kind invitation, but my sister and I are with my father and we will have to speak to him about it first." They moved across the room to where their father sat.

As William thought about her statement he responded, "I would be delighted to meet your father and ask his permission."

Mary and Iris's father was a stately and aristocratic looking man, slightly bald with a huge mustache, and very proper. After the performance, William approached their table and introduced himself to Mary's father. Jack Mitchell was well bred and warmly greeted William. There was just something about William. He could not quite put his finger on it but he liked this young man immediately. Very well bred, William had impeccable manners because of Jane's influence. Mary's strong personality was quite eager but, of course, women's rights had not yet come into fashion and as a single woman, still living in her father's home was very much under his control. They were a very proper family according to the standards of the day. Perhaps that was what he liked so much about William. As a man, and head of his household, Jack, was the typical patriarch. The women who resided there had to have his approval. That is just the way things were in those days before women were more in charge of their own lives and destiny.

Her sister Iris had another view of how women should be in those days. Always feisty and never married she left home at an early age and entered the theatre very much against her parent's wishes. After auditioning and offered a part she joined the Wilson Opera Stock Company. During the early 1900's they toured the US making one-night stands in all forty-eight states performing in all the major theatres of the day. During the women's rights movement, she marched with Susan B. Anthony for the right to vote, and continued to live a long and very active life as a single independent woman. In later years after she left the stage she worked for a well-known newspaper on the mainland until she retired at 75.

It became obvious to Jack that there was a mutual attraction between Mary and William. As they all became more acquainted, William extended an invitation to Jack and his wife, along with Mary and her sister Iris to visit the island before the season came to a close. Delighted with such a lovely invitation, and with a great deal of encouragement from Mary, they accepted. As they completed plans, Jack was very eager to meet William's mother. The scandal his mother had lived through remained an issue. He wondered if there would there be any discussion about that. Mary's family seemed so proper and he wondered if that might become a problem.

Mary and Iris accompanied by their parents traveled through the lovely mountains of Vermont to New Hampshire. As they approached the port where they would take the ferry over to the island, Mary was overwhelmed at the beauty of the local surroundings. They were there to make sure everything was very proper about this meeting. The weather cooperated so the ferry ride went quickly and smoothly. A carriage sent by William was at the dock waiting to drive them to town. Mary was anxious but excited about meeting William's mother and learning more about their family. The scandal, now long forgotten, but always on the tongues of gossipmongers, will be revealed at some point when the time is appropriate.

Jane greeted everyone with a warm welcome. They all gathered around one of the tables in the main dining room. She had prepared tea and home-baked biscuits still hot from oven that she served with her very own fresh-made jam. The conversation was cordial and friendly and Mary could sense that Jane was pleased with the meeting. Jack and Annie Mitchell seemed pleased also as they all reminisced on their trip home. William had just turned 36 and Mary was 33, so they were mature adults. A few days later, in an ongoing family conversation regarding her courtship with William, Mary announced, "Papa, I am not going to be an old maid like Iris!" I want to get married.

After a slow beginning, and many hours together getting to know each other, their courtship became very serious. There were many conversations about marriage and in a short time, with Jane's blessing, and with the permission of her parents Mary and William began making plans for a wedding.

It was somewhat of a long-distance courtship at first, but Mary and William managed to see each other quite often. The scandal was briefly mentioned without all the details. So pleased with their intending marriage, any talk of the scandal was put on a shelf for posterity.

It was agreed that once married the couple would make their home on the island and be part of the Simpson-Camden household at the DuPris Cottage. Jane was delighted that her son, whom she adored, was soon to be married. She approved whole-heartily of this lovely young woman he had chosen. Mary Mitchell was all class and always wore beautiful hand-made hats that matched every outfit, designed and tailored by her. They were married in 1912. A stunning bride she had personally hand-made her entire wedding ensemble. William adoring both his mother and his wife chose a gift of jewelry for each of them to commemorate this special day. His wife received a platinum diamond lovelier and his mother a gold diamond studded broach that could also be worn as a pendant, both originals from Cartier's in New York. Following their marriage, they settled into life at the DuPris Cottage with Jane, now a busy hard-working widow for several years.

William was an active member of the local Masons and soon Mary became involved in the Eastern Star. As a wonderful pianist, she was always sought after to entertain at local events on the island, especially at the Eastern Star and at local Republican functions. William was also quite involved in local politics and eventually became a county committee member for the Republican Party. They seemed to be very well matched and suited to each other.

Since they were approaching their middle years, it was not long before they announced that there was a baby on the way. Expecting another grandchild Jane was delighted and looked forward with great anticipation to the birth. A new generation was about to begin.

Chapter 19

Elizabeth - The New Generation - 1914

Upon entering the kitchen, which was now beautiful and modern, I could only visualize how my mother looked as she cooked on the old coal stove. In the cold winter months we would all gather there. It was always the warmest room in house...

January 24, 1914 was a cold snowy evening and everyone was comfortably seated around the table in the kitchen trying to keep warm when Jane's daughter-in-law Mary Simpson announced that it was time for the baby to come. William, always the kind and gentle man that he was, attended to his wife with compassion to make sure she was comfortable as they waited for a taxi to take them to the local hospital. The baby arrived several hours later, a beautiful healthy baby girl. William was ecstatic. However, some controversy ensued as to the name given to this new little girl. He and his mother wanted one name but Mary did not agree. One name went on the birth certificate, and later legally changed when Elizabeth DuPris Simpson was baptized.

Elizabeth was the apple of her father's eye. He nicknamed her Dolly and took her everywhere with him. The big house was a joyful place with this new little girl growing up, and Jane was enchanted with her beautiful new granddaughter.

Mary introduced eight- year-old Elizabeth to elocution, voice and dance instruction. As she honed her skills, the Eastern Star where her mother was now the Grand Matron, became a showcase for her talent. Her singing, the highlight after their meetings, delighted the entire audience.

During the summer months, the boarders at the DuPris Cottage became her audience. The summer season brought people from all walks of life. One summer as Elizabeth was becoming a stunning young woman, a very famous pianist and composer from New York was a guest at the boarding house. Paul Carmichael completely mesmerized by Elizabeth whose performance delighted all the guests. Now 16 with bright blue eyes and golden blond hair, she was already a beauty, obviously talented and exceptionally trained.

"This was a rare find," Paul thought as he intently observed one of her performances.

Later that evening he cornered William and presented him with a legitimate proposition about a career in the theatre for Elizabeth. Without thinking at all, William emphatically stated, "No! My daughter is not going to go into the theatre." William was very protective of his little girl, who was now becoming a beautiful young woman. But the theatre was not an option for her as far as he was concerned, and that was final.

Elizabeth was maturing into a very lovely and quite attractive young woman. Her high school graduation behind her she decided to attend business school. It was not long before she landed a job at the newspaper, through the help of her Aunt Iris. After leaving the theater, Aunt Iris went to work for a local newspaper on the mainland, and continued to work there for many years until she retired. It was there that Elizabeth eventually met Frank Smith.

Jane, now the matriarch lived and managed the DuPris Cottage along with William, his wife Mary, and her granddaughter Elizabeth. Junior had joined the army so the household remained peaceful and congenial. Since both Mary's parents had recently passed away that left Iris living alone. With Jane's permission, Mary and William encouraged Iris to come and live with them. There was certainly enough room in the house for one more. Continuing to work diligently Jane maintained the DuPris Cottage as a business and a home for the members of her family. There were periods of financial struggle and other difficulties but, for the most part, hours of hard work and happy family times filled their days. Another shadow from the past was soon about to change all that.

Chapter 20

Junior

Looking back to when I was about 12, I remember frequent visits to the DuPris Cottage by Junior, while I was still living there, and how irritated my Mom became when he was around. I also remember visits by the attorney who would eventually handle the contents and outcome of my great-grandmother's Last Will and Testament.

Following his divorce from his teenage bride, Junior floundered for a few years and then joined the army in of 1917. Following service to his country, he is honorably discharged in March 1919. Returning home he has nowhere to turn but to Jane. Unoccupied, the bungalow once again becomes his refuge for a small monthly sum. Having served in the war and acquired a bit of maturity, he learned to avoid the big house and allowed the rest of the family and the guests some privacy.

Because of his training in the army, he became an engineer, and that gave him some stability and provided him with income. Jane and the rest of the family not pleased, he began to court his cousin. They were second cousins and that seemed inappropriate to everyone. Clara DuPris was single, young and attractive and the daughter of Jane's brother. Junior was several years her senior and always had his eye on her. Once again, Jane was very much against his choice for a wife. The bloodline was much too close for comfort and that was most certainly not to her liking. But Junior defied his grandmother once again, and anyone else who attempted to counsel him on the issue. He married her in spite of everyone's objections and, in the years that followed, he seemed to settle down with this new wife. As time passed, he eventually acquired an excellent reputation as an extremely competent engineer on the island. He and his wife seemed to enjoy living a quiet life and had several children.

Junior continued to stay in touch with his grandmother but learned to keep his distance from the big house where she still lived with her son William, and his family members. Without Junior's presence, the DuPris cottage remained a happy peaceful place.

One morning, in a discussion with William Jane, now getting on in years decided she was going to have her will drawn up. Of course, her son William would be the beneficiary. However, when Junior's name came up, William's heart skipped a beat. Even though Junior's life seemed to be going well, he never let Jane forget her promise of a house. Always trying to do the right thing, she decided to make him a co-beneficiary along with William, never suspecting what problems that might cause in the future. After some discussion, William agreed. Perhaps it would aid in keeping Junior satisfied knowing that he would be in her will. Little did she or William anticipate the effect that such a decision would have on the future of the family, an effect that would continue long after her death and the probating of her Will.

Chapter 21

Jane's Final Days

As I walked around the cottage on a bleak rainy day, I sat down in Jane's favorite rocking chair once again. Looking at her photograph, I could see how she appeared in her golden years and I began to wonder how her life ended...

Jane may have had a premonition of things to come, thus the Will. A few years later, during the winter of 1935, there was quite a bad snowstorm. The streets were covered with ice and snow for several weeks. Although now in her late seventies and healthy, Jane, still very independent was well known and admired as an active member of the community. She was a member of the Lady's Society at the local church and was still extremely active in the Eastern Star. One morning, as she walked the main street in town to attend a church meeting she slipped and fell on the ice and broke her hip. Some local businesspeople saw her fall and called an ambulance. William was notified and quickly rushed to the hospital. He worried so about his mother and visited her often, during her confinement over the next several weeks.

Having lots of time to think, while lying in the hospital bed, she began to recall all the events of her life. Struggling at different times and facing numerous hardships, she felt extremely proud of the fact she survived so well.

Her first thoughts drifted to the past and her first meeting with Jonathan and how, in her innocence she had succumbed to his manipulations. Even so, her heart fluttered as she remembered some of their very tender moments together. It was young love and you only experience that once in life. Her memory still very acute, she recalled how passionately they made love that first time. It had ended badly, but her recollection of those first moments remained.

As her thoughts turn to Harry and their years together, she smiled knowing those had been her best years. Even though they struggled at times, there were so many happy events to look back on. She recalled their many tender moments: their first trip to the inn in New Hampshire when Harry had first confessed his love for her and all their intimate moments; working together in the hotel and their many successful business partnerships. Theirs was a mature love based on mutual respect. She pondered their years together, and the stresses of their relationship, she remembered his strength, his tenderness with her and how he had loved and cared for her children. As she recalled the loss of their child, tears welled up in her eyes and began to roll town her cheeks…she still missed both of them so! When some of life's tragedies leave such scars, the wounds never seem to heal. Recalling Harry's presence, she knew he had profoundly changed her life. She was so grateful for that.

Wiping away the tears, she felt at peace and was pleased with what she had accomplished. She always remained a strong independent women and the matriarch of her family all of her life. In a time when women were so dependent on a man for their livelihood she, as a widow, succeeded in running a thriving business and in her will was able to leave a small estate to her loved ones. The end came several weeks later when Jane contracted pneumonia. Lovingly at her side, William was with her when she passed peacefully in March 1935. Her legacy will live on and the future generations will be inspired by her courage and fortitude.

William had been her constant companion as a child during the troublesome years with Jonathan. Clinging and depending on him as she aged they had a close and wonderful relationship all through her life, and especially during her golden years. She had told him on so many occasions that she was so proud of him. This kind and gentle man was now grief stricken. His wife Mary, always at his side provided weeks of support and comfort as he learned to adjust to life without his Mom.

A memorial service was held in the local church where Jane was a member. Filled to capacity where she had been a constant presence, the church had become a respite for her after Harry's passing. It had given her great comfort, as well as her involvement in the local political activities, where she found so much joy working for the community. Jane's interment in the cemetery adjacent to the church that she had attended most of her life brings tears to many in attendance. Any scandal about her life long forgotten, she will lie peacefully beside her beloved Harry, their son

Tommy and her daughter. The local paper published an extensive obituary about her life. Her commitment and work in the community will be remembered for years to come and will be greatly missed.

Several weeks went by before the reading of her Will. However, it would be a number of years before the Will is probated. Even though Junior was not in touch with the family for several years, he promptly showed up at the funeral, and for the reading of Jane's last Will and Testament. Two pieces of jewelry were left as part of her estate. She bequeathed a gold diamond studded broach to her granddaughter Elizabeth. To the local church where she had been a member all her adult life, she left a substantial donation. The rest of her estate divided between William and Junior, included the DuPris Cottage, the bungalow in the rear of the house and the retail store. Long past the time of her death, and the reading and probating of her Will, its contents created unending arguments and contentiousness. Junior continued to contribute nothing but heartache to all concerned. In the weeks and years that followed, he harassed William relentlessly, wanting to claim his inheritance. Many issues were raised as a result and that caused hours upon hours of arguments between William and Junior. Naturally, Mary and Elizabeth would side with William and became very upset every time Junior showed up unannounced. Rightfully, he had a claim, but William and his family were currently the inhabitants of the big house, except for a few short months in the summer, when it was still run as a boarding house. As the summer months rolled around, they would always move into the bungalow in the rear of the main house.

The revenue from the boarding house and the antique store gave Mary and William, now entering their senior years, additional funds to supplement what meager income William was receiving from social security and his pension from the fire department.

The acrimony between Elizabeth and Junior became very disturbing to her mom and dad. Elizabeth adored her father and was very protective of him as he was of her. He and Junior were not able to be in the same room without having words about the Will. Showing up without notice from time to time, attempting to coerce William into moving out or selling the property so that he could realize the money from the sale. "Possession is nine tenths of the law," William would always say, since he and his family occupied the big house. Naturally, this comment only added to Junior's anger and frustration. On several occasions, he also attempted at trying to get a financial settlement equal to his share from William, but without success. There was really no money available for any type of settlement. William and Mary had minimal resources and survived on a very meager income. Eventually forced to hire a lawyer, Josh Goldberg was now handling the entire estate issue so that William would not have to deal personally with Junior anymore. William was getting on in years and Junior's presence always upset him and drove his blood pressure sky high.

On one occasion, Junior threatened to have William, Mary, Aunt Iris and Elizabeth evicted. Always with that sense of entitlement, he seemed determined to force the issue. His attorney suggested that the property be sold so he could claim his inheritance. However, deep inside

Junior knew that was never going to happen. Having no compassion for their situation, he disregarded what effect it might have on three people in their golden years, and Elizabeth who is now a young woman. He wanted to have his way, or else. Nevertheless, William's attorney was never going to allow any of those scenarios to take place.

Chapter 22

Elizabeth Meets Jack Cole

I was drawn to the very large formal dining room where the kids were banging on the piano. Loving the sound of a piano and having learned to play in my senior years I scolded them and told them to stop. They ran out of the room giggling. So I sat down and began to play one of my favorites. As I finished and remained sitting there in a kind of meditative state, I wondered how many different people had eaten in that room, as it was used by all the guests, when the cottage was operated as a boarding house. However, mostly I was reminded that my mother and father's wedding reception had taken place in that room....

Now, a stunning young beauty, Elizabeth captured the attention of many of the single men on the island. She became engaged to a young man Frank Smith whom she met at the newspaper where she was working, and it appeared that they might marry. Their relationship lasted seven years but Elizabeth ended it abruptly when she met Jack Cole.

He had just completed his college years with degrees in Civil Engineering and Architecture, but the country was still recovering from the depression. Even though he graduated with honors, work was hard to come by. He eventually went to work for a very small salary, under a program that was part of FDR's New Deal.

One afternoon in 1939, while Jack was walking along the beach with one of his college buddie's, he noticed a beautiful blonde young woman coming toward them, escorted by a pleasant looking man. His eyes became glued to her. Suddenly in a visionary moment he turned to his friends and stated emphatically and without reservation, "You see that beautiful girl there...well I am going to marry her one day!" As they all laughed, he wondered to himself, "What made me say that?"

Not too long after that, a mutual friend coincidentally introduced them at a local dance. Upon meeting Elizabeth, Jack wondered if God was having a hand in this. It seemed like such a coincidence. Being a math major he knew that coincidence meant to coincide. Was the universe creating a sort of dance of love? No matter what was happening Jack was pleased and asked her for a dance. Elizabeth was immediately attracted to Jack's handsome good looks. The first time he waltzed her around the floor she was quite smitten. Jack was a wonderful dancer and Elizabeth loved to dance. It seemed like love at first sight for them both. Jack did not waste any time asking for a first date. In no time at all, they became inseparable and were being propelled toward a future together.

During her next evening out with Frank, Elizabeth informed him as gently as possible that she was ending their relationship. "I have met someone else and I can't see you anymore Frank." Frank was in shock and tried to change her mind. She was adamant, "Look Frank, you will find someone else, anyway after seven-years I don't think our relationship is really going anywhere. And besides, there are plenty more fish in the sea." "That may be true," he replied, "but they are not all gold ones!" As that conversation ended, Frank and Elizabeth parted and never saw each other again.

Elizabeth and Jack became inseparable, socialized often with some of the other couples from the island and seemed to have an active life. During their months of courtship, he wrote a song in her honor, entitled "I Met a Girl". Within a short time, they fell hopelessly in love and after dating for less than a year, they were discussing the possibility of marriage. One night, while out for the evening, they arrived home very late at the DuPris Cottage. Elizabeth's parents were out in front of the house pacing up and down waiting for them. "Where have you been till this hour?" her father insisted. Elizabeth now 25 and feeling like an adult, was embarrassed and appalled at their attitude. They actually scolded her and demanded that she come inside. As an obedient daughter, she reluctantly did as she was asked. Being their only child, they were always overly protective of her. She was angry, but as time passed, she learned to forgive them

William recalling his mother's history was always worried about any new young man Elizabeth went out with, and the fact that she might be manipulated into improper behavior. Thankfully, Elizabeth was a strong and intelligent young woman and was not about to let that happen. Besides Jack was a devout Catholic, having been educated in all Catholic schools. He was very careful not to break any church laws about intimacy before marriage. With time and in the end William and Mary were pleased and became quite fond of Jack Cole. He came from a good family that was well known on the island. His father Patrick, a stationary engineer, came through Ellis Island as an Irish immigrant and later naturalized as a U.S. citizen. His mother Jenny was born in New York. Jack was college educated and a very bright young man. They became confident that their only daughter's future would be in good hands.

Always planning romantic surprises, when the one-year anniversary of the day they met arrived, Jack showed up at her front door with an adorable puppy. When Elizabeth answered the door, she was surprised to see Jack holding a dog in his arms. It did not take long for that surprised look to become a huge smile, when she discovered a diamond ring hanging from the collar around the dog's neck. Jack quickly handed her the puppy so that he could remove the ring, and slide it on her finger. With all the commotion and the puppy barking her parents showed up at the door to see what all the excitement was. Elizabeth abruptly handed the dog to her Dad and threw her arms around Jack's neck. With excitement and an outpouring of emotion, she knew what this meant.

A lovely wedding was soon being planned. Jack's sister Anne, whom he was very close to, was chosen to be the maid of honor, and one of his college friend's was to be best man. The Coles's were a well-known Catholic family on the island. Not wanting her to have two religions in her family, Elizabeth's mother Mary, in her wisdom, encouraged her daughter to become a Catholic. Elizabeth decided to follow her Mother's advice. She and Jack were married at the local Catholic Church, and 100 guests were invited to the reception, which was held in the large formal dining room of the DuPris Cottage. At the close of the festivities, the couple departed on their wedding trip to Washington, DC.

Returning from a weeklong honeymoon, they settled into the routine of married life. Elizabeth embraced the Catholic faith that she had adopted, and as a couple, they devoutly practiced the Catholic religion. A lovely apartment near the big house, redecorated by her mother, was waiting for them. Not practicing birth control according to Catholic doctrine, ten months later a daughter Amanda was born. A frequent visitor, Anne was chosen to be the godmother and carry on the Catholic education of the new baby, if it became necessary. Not having children herself, she was ecstatic about her role and this new addition to the family. Anne Cole, a smart and very independent woman, was an officer and head teller at the local bank, and had never married. During the depression years, Jack was in college and she was the only member of Jack's family working. She helped keep the Cole's in an adequate financial position, during some times of great scarcity and hardship.

It was October 1940 and while there was much new activity and joy about this new baby girl, the newspaper headlines kept everyone on edge. A war was brewing in Europe and it appeared the U.S. eventually might be involved in it. Jack and Elizabeth settled into a relatively quiet life style enjoying their new little girl. Jack continued to work in a WPA works project. Hardly recovered from Amanda's birth Elizabeth found herself pregnant again. With the coming of another new baby and the possibility of a war, the couple moved into the big house with Elizabeth's mom, dad and aunt, so the family could all be together. Less than one year later a new baby boy, Ted, becomes part of the household.

Although Jack was a very bright college graduate, he found work to be sporadic with low pay. The country was still feeling some effects of the great depression and jobs were still scarce. The move to the big house allowed them to save money for their future, and effectively reduced living costs for all concerned.

In early 1943, at the height of the war, Elizabeth gave birth to a third baby, their second boy, Jack, Jr.

When August 1945 rolled around, there was a huge celebration out in the streets as the war officially ended. At the time, Amanda now approaching the age of five was very puzzled. She wondered why everyone was so happy and excited. In the years to come she will learn the answer to that question. As the country began to heal, the family resumed a quiet routine for the next couple of years.

In the fall of 1948, Jack, Elizabeth and the three children returned from a long vacation in the northeast. Two weeks later Amanda was diagnosed with Polio, and the house was quarantined for 21 days. Amanda was confined to a hospital and remained there for the next three months. There was so much fear about Polio that neighbors and friends completely avoided the family. The two boys remained home from school and felt so isolated since their playmates were kept at a distance. Without Amanda's presence, the household atmosphere was somewhat somber. Elizabeth, a constant worrier, kept in touch with the hospital as much as possible, while tending to normal household chores and the two boys. Both Jack and Elizabeth visited their precious daughter each Sunday for a short time, according to the extreme curatorial guidelines of the hospital. Amanda was a good patient and seemed reconciled to her fate, even though she longed to go home with them as each visit concluded. It was very emotional and difficult for them to leave her there, but her strong, courageous attitude seemed to ease the discomfort they felt.

Shortly before Christmas, a phone call came from the hospital that Amanda was to be released. Immediately, Elizabeth hired a taxi and was at the hospital before an hour had passed. Amanda's room all ready for this day, Elizabeth was not going to wait a minute longer to bring her little girl home. It would be a special Christmas.

Christmas in the big house was always a happy and festive celebration. Up most of the night on Christmas Eve Jack would be singing or whistling carols as he meticulously decorated the tree, placing every ornament and light precisely where he wanted them. Living close by on the island his family was always included in all the holiday festivities. Jack's father had already passed but his mother and two sisters, both of whom were independent women and had remained unmarried, enjoyed many happy times being part of the DuPris-Simpson-Camden family during those years.

One Christmas, as the entire family gathered together stands out above all the rest. Jack surprised Amanda with a playhouse, built by him and large enough that she could go into it. Painted bright red, it was one room with a table and chair all set for tea, and even a play telephone. After a big turkey dinner with all the trimmings, prepared to perfection by Elizabeth, everyone opened lots of presents. At the close of day before everyone departed for home, Mary would go to the piano and play carols and songs that everyone knew. Everyone sang along. Amanda and the boys always wanted to sing solos, and so they were encouraged to do so. It was there very early Amanda's life that her love of singing had its roots, Jack loved to sing the kids to sleep each night. Both Jack and Elizabeth had grown up with music and someone always playing the piano. They were both offered opportunities to go into the entertainment business, but chose the traditional life of work and raising a family.

When the holidays ended, life slowly returned to a sense of normalcy. Amanda, Ted and Jack Jr. were finally all back in school and growing. With the coming of summer, the family moved into the bungalow behind the big house and as tradition would have it, the DuPris Cottage was made ready for the ensuing hordes of guests, and once again run as a boarding house for the season. Throughout the season and particularly at its close there were lots of parties, piano playing, and singing. Amanda always managed a way to be part of all those parties, and participated in the singing of all the old songs. The kids were always excited. The summer brought lots of new faces, especially new playmates who came with their parents to stay in the Cottage. As each summer came to a close, and with the arrival of fall, the family moved back into the big house. This became a yearly ritual.

From time to time Junior would eventually show up again and harass William about his share of the inheritance. He continued to come and go for several years, and so did the letters from his attorney. All it accomplished was increased debt owed to William's attorney who was compelled to respond to the letters, and postpone any kind of settlement. Junior's presence always unnerved Elizabeth. Amanda, although young and not understanding all the issues involved, became quite upset at her mother's reaction to Junior. She witnessed them having harsh words on several occasions. Elizabeth, of course, was just trying to protect her dad, but to no avail. The energy that remained due to Junior's presence and departure left everyone feeling poorly and irritable, after every visit.

Due to Jane's decision, and the Will she had left behind, this dark shadow continued to lurk over the Simpson household for years.

Part Two

Amanda

I have a dream...
Dream and it might come true....
Dreams can create magical moments
So, never give up your dreams!

Chapter 23

Déjà vu

Up until now, I have avoided the bedroom at the top of the stairs. However, I am being beckoned to the one unforgettable shadow in my life that comes to mind about that room. Arriving on the second floor, I enter the bedroom that had once belonged to my mom and dad. As I did an unfamiliar feeling came over me, and I had to lie down on the bed. After lying there for, I was not sure how long; I drifted off into what seemed like some kind of a dream state. Suddenly it felt like I was a little girl again, lying in my mother and father's big bed. It seemed like I was sick but I did not feel too bad, just a headache and a stiff neck...

1948

Dr. Nelson asked Elizabeth to step outside the bedroom into the hall to where her mother, Mary and Aunt Iris were anxiously waiting to hear his diagnosis. Amanda, the beautiful hazel-eyed daughter of Elizabeth and Jack Cole lay listless in her parents' large bed. (Elizabeth always let the children sleep in her big bed when they were sick.)

"It's either Polio or Spinal Meningitis," he told Elizabeth, "and a spinal tap needs to be done to determine which it is."

Elizabeth's heart felt as though it was not going to beat again. Her hands and the back of her neck became sweaty. Feelings of vertigo seem to overwhelm her as Dr. Nelson's words drifted through her thoughts. She moved a few steps and leaned against the wall hoping it would keep her from falling. Mary and Aunt Iris gasped when they heard Polio!

It was the fall of 1948. The Cole's had just returned from an extended vacation in the northeast and Canada. It was a happy time for all of them. The children were growing and healthy, and finally in school. Having given birth to three babies in three years, the previous years had been hectic, especially for Elizabeth. Things were easier now but the children remained the center of Elizabeth's life. Each child in his or her own way had completely captured her heart.

Jack Cole was a scholar, an incurable romantic, and quite a handsome man with dark brown wavy hair, and eyes that changed color. His love for Elizabeth was unbounded. She was a beautiful blue-eyed blonde-haired woman, and the daughter of one of the well-known families, on this picturesque island off the coastlines of Maine and New Hampshire. Jack Cole's family, also quite well known, lived on the island too. They were from upper class Irish immigrants.

Elizabeth's family owned the boarding house on Seagull Beach Drive, which is where they had received their wedding guests. It sat high above the heart of town on a hill overlooking the ocean. Nicknamed the "big house" by the family, because there was also a small bungalow (the "little house") that sat just behind the main house. Adjacent, on the same property, was a retail store rented to an antique dealer that gave the family additional income.

The big house, an old Victorian known as "The DuPris Cottage" was built in 1892 with a huge wrap-around porch; it had two sets of double leaded class front doors. One set led to a huge formal dining room that could accommodate 100 guests, the other set led to the main parlor. There were twenty-four rooms on three floors, a huge kitchen with an old coal stove that helped to keep everyone warm in the cold months of winter, a main floor lavatory and pantry, a parlor, a smaller family dining room, 15 bedrooms and three bathrooms; with a couple of smaller rooms in the attic.

Elizabeth's father, William DuPris Simpson moved there when he was just six months old, and lived there all his life. He was considered a pioneer on that island. In earlier years his mother, Jane DuPris, had owned it and ran it as a boarding house. The cottage and its inhabitants were well known on the island. When William married Mary Mitchell, they resided there with his mother Jane. Their only child, Elizabeth was born and raised there.

During the war years, Jack and Elizabeth lived with them along with Amanda and the two boys, Ted and Jack, Jr. All the children's early years were spent growing up there. A music lover, Jack enjoyed singing the children to sleep every night as he put them to bed. Elizabeth's mother Mary, was an accomplished pianist and her sister Iris, who had been in the theatre for many years, had moved in with them a few years before, so the household was continuously filled with music, singing and play-acting.

As Elizabeth regained her composure and Dr. Nelson's words began to sink in, her mind was in a fog as to what needed to be done.

Aware of her anxious state, Dr. Nelson comforted her, "Don't worry Elizabeth; I will make all the arrangements. She will have to go to a special hospital that treats infectious diseases where they can do the spinal tap, and we will need to quarantine the entire household for about 21 days. When we know the result of the spinal tap we will know how to treat her."

Dr. Nelson, who delivered Amanda and was a family friend, came to see her twice on the day Elizabeth received the dreaded diagnosis that her little girl was a victim of Polio. Amanda told him that her neck was stiff and she had a headache. He took her temperature, touched the back of her neck and then disappeared out into the hall where Amanda could barely hear him talking to her mother.

Lying in her parent's big bed, Amanda dozed in and out of sleep most of that day. When she woke up and looked out the window, she noticed it was starting to get dark. There was a lot of commotion going on downstairs. Lots of voices, blended, it was difficult to tell whom they were or what they were saying. Then, like a herd of elephants, they came up the stairs. Amanda watched as they all paraded into the bedroom, including a bald headed man that she did not know, wearing a long white coat. She soon learned he was another doctor that her father's family had brought in to confirm the diagnosis. After an hour of testing, he arrived at the same conclusion. Preparation was then begun to transport her to the hospital where they would do the spinal tap.

Amanda seemed to have lost track of time as she was removed from her mother and father's bed and transferred to a taxi, accompanied by both parents. The night sky was clear and she noticed the full moon out the window of the taxi. It seemed somewhat mystical and made her feel uncomfortable as she watched a lonely cloud pass over it. When the car stopped, Jack Cole lifted his precious little girl from the car and carried her through a very large door. Waiting inside the entrance to the hospital there was a large gurney. A strange odor permeated the air as she was being rolled down a long hallway, and the huge lights down the center of the ceiling had been dimmed since it was now late at night. It was quiet, almost eerie, and she could sense a nurse and a doctor just behind her head briskly wheeling her to, she was not sure where. They were talking quietly to each other, almost whispering, so she could not make out what they were saying. As they entered a cold brightly lit room, they placed the gurney under a large light. It was so bright that Amanda wanted to close her eyes, but then she was suddenly lifted up and turned on her stomach. She felt something cold and damp on her lower back. The nurse said, "Now don't move till we tell you it's all right." There was lot of noise and moving about in the room. A spinal tap was performed confirming that she had Polio. Thankfully, she didn't seem to experience any discomfort during the procedure. Because of this diagnosis, the doctor decided to have her admitted.

When everything quieted down, they were once again in motion, going down another long hall. They entered a very large room painted light green with many glass partitions. In between each partition was a bed and nightstand. Amanda wondered if one of them was for her when suddenly she was lifted off the gurney into a bed. The nurse said, "You rest now dear" and left. Suddenly, her parents appeared at the side of her bed. She sensed her mother's anxiety but her dad was calm and controlled, with an air of concern. She remained stoic not wanting to cry. They told her to be a good girl and said they had to leave but promised to be back soon. She noticed her mother's eyes welling up with tears, but not wanting to upset Amanda, Elizabeth resisted the urge to cry. The nurse came in to escort them out and then they were gone.

Alone now with only her thoughts, Amanda was trying to make seven-year old sense out what had just happened to her. It was dark and quiet with only scattered ribbons of light coming in from the hallway. Eventually, she drifted off to sleep and the next day when she awoke the sun was shining, but she really did not feel sick at all. For a split second she had forgotten the events of the previous evening and thought it was time to get up for school. As she suddenly noticed the green walls and the glass partition that surrounded her bed, it all came back to her. She was in the hospital, and alone. Her parents were nowhere in sight, only nurses and other children who were also patients. Some of them were beginning to get up and move about. A nurse approached her and said, "Good morning Amanda. How are you feeling today, dear?" She just stared at her not answering, but wondering what would be next.

As she scanned the room, she noticed other children with braces on their legs, or some deformity in one of their arms. Some were bedridden and others were in these big machines that made a loud thumping noise. She began to discover they were Iron Lungs, helping the occupants to breathe. It should have occurred to her that she should feel very fortunate to have the Polio bug located in her back where it did not manifest any signs paralysis, but it did not. She would discover that knowledge years later but all she knew at the time was that she wanted to go home.

Within a few days, she became friends with some of the other children, and that seemed to make it easier to be there. Over the next few months while, physically feeling totally normal, she often wondered, "Why am I here so long?"

Feeling well with no signs of illness or disability she and the other kids often had too much time on their hands. Boredom occasionally led to mischievous behavior. Many of the children with no paralysis were up and about as if they were totally well and healthy. On a cold rainy day, bored to tears, some of the kids were running down the hall laughing. As they passed the elevators, a voice came from the back of the group, "Let's go for a ride on the elevator." With excitement in his voice another one yelled, "Ill push the button and when the elevator comes let's all get in and go up to the third floor." "Ok", everyone agreed. They had not noticed the two nurses at the end of the hall keeping an eye on them, but that did not stop them. Suddenly the doors opened and they all just stood there for a moment wondering if they should really get on. Then all at once they moved together and could hardly get through the door! It played like an old comedy movie.

One of the boys pushed number three and up they went. Before they reached the third floor the elevator came to a screeching halt and bounced up and down; boredom and, what they all thought would be fun, quickly turned to fright. The elevator was stuck between floors. Someone yelled, "What should we do now?" A girl in the back with panic in her voice yelled, "Push the bell so someone will come and help us, hurry up!" The bell was so loud they could not hear anything but a loud clanking noise. After, what seemed like forever, the elevator started back down again and stopped with a huge bounce? When the doors opened the two nurses were standing there and seemed to be ready to scold everyone, but instead they started laughing. Seeing the kids get on the elevator they decided to teach them all a lesson. They actually had stopped the elevator to scare the kids so they would not do it again… and it worked because during the rest of Amanda's stay in the hospital all the kids stayed far from the elevators.

Several weeks later workers began coming, going and moving the beds around. Wondering what was happening, the kids gathered around one of the nurses. "What's going on?" one of the girls asked. Miss Spiro replied, "It's time to paint the girl's ward and you are all going to be staying in the boy's ward for a couple of days." All the girls moaned with disappointment. The next day they were all moved and crowded into the boy's ward. They ran out of beds and since Amanda was one of the youngest and extremely petite, they put her in a crib. Insulted is not quite the word for how she felt; she was downright indignant. She thought, "How could they put me into a crib? After all I am not a baby; I am all grown up now and just had my eighth birthday!"

Polio was contagious and in 1948, very little was known about how to treat it. Physical exercise was the most important factor of the treatment. Three times per day a nurse would give Amanda an injection of Curare, a poison used by the South American Indians on their blow darts. It was a dangerous drug and caused weakness of the skeletal muscles. An overdose could cause death. However, it was used with great caution to allow the physical therapist to administer exercising of all muscles, with a minimum amount of discomfort. Amanda's spine and back were affected by the virus so there was no paralysis of her limbs.

Amanda had very little contact with her parents during her stay in the hospital. The glass partition that surrounded her bed was like a barricade between she and her parents, when they came to visit. Allowed to visit only once a week for a half hour wearing white gowns and facemasks, they came, religiously, every Sunday. Elizabeth worried and worried so about her little girl during that period. So many times through the years, Amanda would remember her mother saying that she had aged ten years during the months her little girl was in the hospital.

Although, in her heart she knew it was not true, Amanda had always felt as if she was being detained in some kind of prison, and did not understand why.

Thoughts of running away surfaced now and again. Then the day finally came for her to go home, and she was free.

After a three-month confinement, where she had matured to the ripe old age of eight, Amanda returned home to her family completely well, feeling like she had never even been sick. Nevertheless, the doctors required her to continue physical therapy for the next three years.

A lovely bedroom all her own, entirely re-decorated by Elizabeth for her little girl, was waiting for Amanda as she arrived home. This was a special day for the family, although the days ahead were to be somewhat challenging. Amanda had changed in many ways during her confinement in a hospital. She had actually matured beyond her eight years and learned to be very self-sufficient. At times, her parents seemed puzzled by her, and were not sure how to handle her. One day she overheard her mom telling her grandmother Mary, "Amanda went away a little girl but came home an adult."

The entire experience, learning to be on her own and the feelings of independence she gained would enrich her life and benefit her all through her adult years, as we shall learn.

Chapter 24

William's Legacy

Very well known as an early inhabitant of the island, my grandfather, William spent many hours with us. I nicknamed him "Bompa" at the tender age of three. He called me Dolly, the same term of endearment that he had bestowed on my mother. Every morning he would rise early, put the coffee on and then take a short trip to the local grocery store for rolls and sweet buns. He prepared special coffee for all of us. Sugar rationing was in place so he sweetened the coffee with condensed milk.

Lifting me high above his head and placing me on his shoulders, we would take a walk to the local bookie so he could place a bet on the horse of the day. How he loved the horses! He listened intently to the races on the radio and there was always a daily racing form lying around. My recollection of the bookie is even clear as a bell to this day; he was a large stately man with a huge handlebar mustache. Always decked out in a white suit and a straw hat, he would look at me and say "Hello dolly," with a huge smile, as he chewed on a big fat cigar. As I look back on these special moments with my grandfather it was no wonder that I cried uncontrollably, as I rode in the car to his interment.

Elizabeth, Jack and the children continued to live on in the big house with Elizabeth's Mom, Dad and Aunt Iris for a few more years. In 1952, they began to think about having a home of their own. As they began their search, it led them to a lovely place on the mainland where they started a new life.

With the children and grandkids gone William, Mary and Aunt Iris enjoyed a more peaceful household, but they missed the kids terribly. Elizabeth, Jack and the children visited often and they always all gathered at the big house for the Thanksgiving and Christmas holidays, along with Jack's family.

Junior, still adamant about the right to his inheritance, continued to pay unwelcomed visits now and then.

Then one day William complained of shortness of breath and much discomfort. Mary called Dr. Nelson and he stopped by for a visit later that day. Oxygen was ordered for him to have in the house at his disposal all the time.

Due to smoke inhalation from all the years working for the fire department, William's health was beginning to deteriorate. Provided with oxygen by the local fire department, he eventually had to use it constantly. Not knowing what might happen in the future, he contacted his attorney to review his will, so that Mary would not have to deal with Junior once he was gone. In his final days, a codicil to his original Will was drawn up. All his worldly possessions are left to Mary, with a provision for Junior, if the estate was ever sold.

During the cold winter of 1954 in his 78th year, William became gravely ill with pneumonia. Breathing problems had contributed to a heart issue. Now with pneumonia, his poor health was rapidly declining and he had to be hospitalized. He hated the food and constantly insisted on being allowed to go home. Diligently Mary brought him home-cooked meals much to the objection of the hospital personnel. She too was a strong independent woman, much like William's mother, and no one was going to keep her from feeding her husband tasty nutritious meals. William became so agitated about going home the hospital personnel were forced to strap him to the bed to keep him from getting up and leaving. The following day finding William strapped to the bed, Mary demanded to take him home so he could be peaceful and receive her care and good food. Dr. Nelson granted her wishes and she brought him home. With Elizabeth and her family now in a home of their own, Mary redecorated the smaller family dining room into a comfortable first-floor bedroom for William so he no longer had to climb the stairs. A hospital bed and several tanks of oxygen were provided by the local fire department.

Only weeks later, Aunt Iris awakened early and went down for breakfast to find that he had peacefully passed away during the night. Immediately Iris called to Mary to come quickly. Throwing on a robe, she rushed down the stairs. Aunt Iris greeted her at the bottom of the stairs, and reached for her to tell her that William has passed away. Disbelieving what Iris told her, she quickly went to his room and sat down on the side of the bed. Suddenly, realizing that it was true she took his, already cold hand in hers and tears began to run down her cheeks. An hour or more passed as she remembered their love and the years that had gone by. Suddenly, a loud knock at the front door brought her back to the present. Aunt Iris had immediately called Elizabeth and gently told her of her father's passing. Picking up the children from school Elizabeth arrived as quickly as possible to comfort her mother and help prepare for a funeral.

Including the children at the wake and the funeral, is a decision Elizabeth would come to regret in later years. Nine years old at the time Jack, Jr. was bothered by nightmares for weeks after seeing his grandfather dead in the casket.

In the limousine on the way to the cemetery, Amanda sat next to her grandmother. Grieving and remembering events about her husband, Mary kept talking incessantly about things from the past. Stirred with emotion as she listened to her grandmother, Amanda was prompted to lay her head in her grandmother's lap where she began to cry uncontrollably. At the gravesite, as she watched her grandfather's casket lowered into the ground, her heart was breaking. He was interred near where he had buried his mother and her Harry.

Grief stricken after William passed Mary continued to live on in the big house for several months with her sister. Then one day a certified letter came advising Mary that the local town government on the island wanted to purchase the DuPris cottage. It needed a lot of updating so this came at the perfect time since two elderly women were no longer able to care for this large house alone. Plans for another type of housing to be erected on the property were in the works. Due to the provisions of William's will and with the pending sale of the cottage to the government, Junior would finally realize a small inheritance. Not pleased with the terms of the will he wanted more than what was offered. However, his attorney encouraged him to accept it. He really had no other choice.

With her Dad gone, Elizabeth and Jack decided to have Mary and Aunt Iris live with them rather than remain alone in the big house, knowing they would soon be forced to vacate. Delighted they began to plan for the move. Nineteen hundred fifty-four was ending and the kids were excited to have Nana and Aunt Iris coming to live with them just in time for the family to be together for Christmas.

Over the next few weeks, they moved into Elizabeth's home with a minimum amount of belongings. Most of the furniture was left in the big house along with some antiques. The Cole's home was fully furnished except for a couple of extra beds and dressers that Mary and Aunt Iris brought with them. In all the confusion, several photos and memorabilia were inadvertently left behind. The house was closed up waiting for the local government to tear it down.

Then early one morning a few months later while reading the local paper, Mary was shocked as she read an article saying that the DuPris cottage was being acquired by the local historical society. Since it had always been a landmark on the island, they had lobbied to save and restore it. Mary called everyone to the kitchen to announce what she had just read. Knowing that the house where they had all shared so many wonderful family memories and events would not be destroyed, there were cheers of happiness.

As Mary and Aunt Iris settled into their new life, they became quite active in the local Presbyterian Church where they made many friends. Every week on Wednesday afternoon, they would go to bible study and then to church on Sunday morning. Elizabeth, Jack and the children attended mass at the local Catholic Church.

Amanda and her grandmother Mary shared a bedroom together creating a very close relationship over the next few years. Being a strong woman with great insight and intuition, Mary had great influence on Amanda. She was always fascinated by the fact that Mary could read palms, was somewhat physic, and had such wisdom.

Shopping with her grandmother Amanda always returned home with not one, but many new outfits. Whenever Amanda needed a dress for a special occasion or a school dance Mary came to her rescue, just as she had when she was a little girl when they lived in the big house. Extremely wise and loving beautiful clothes she became a wonderful role model and mentor for Amanda in many ways.

Many of Amanda's dreams of performing one day were influenced by Mary and Aunt Iris's real life stories of the theater. Amanda's early life experience in the hospital on her own at age seven, and living under the same roof with these two strong and wise older women were indeed an education for Amanda. In addition, the effect of their musical knowledge and talent would affect many of her lifelong dreams, desires and future choices, as we shall see. The one memory that will live in her heart forever is the love, kindness and compassion of all her family members, especially those of her Mother and Father. She recalled how much they unconditionally loved and cared for each of their three children.

Chapter 25

1953 - 1983 Amanda

Amanda and her brothers were growing up rapidly as their lives return to a more normal routine. Relocating the year Amanda turned twelve meant a new school and new friends. She was always smart in school right from her first year, which made this transition easy. Special events like singing her first solo on the stage at age six was to influence her future. She made friends easily and enjoyed school. Growing up in a musical family, she always loved to sing, dance and perform. All through elementary school, she was involved in several school plays or musical shows.

In high school, she sang in the chorus, was in the drama club, and became a cheerleader for football and basketball. She learned to oil paint in art class and even landed a small part in the senior play. Her dreams and hopes of a career singing in the theatre were locked away in her heart. Her high school years seemed to fly by. There were football games, cheerleading, parties, dances and boyfriends.

Being raised in a strict Catholic family she attended church regularly, but was not totally convinced of the "truth" of all the doctrine and dogma. These doubts would surface often and continued into her adult life.

One boy, her only steady boyfriend during her high school years, made a significant impression on her. She met him at a summer dance party just prior to her senior year. His name was Danny. He was extremely intelligent, philosophical, a great dancer and adorable! He was her "first love". They had an intense relationship for two teenagers. One might say that they were in love. They spent all their spare moments together. In one memorable quiet alone moment, one the beach with his head in her lap, he looked into her eyes and said, "I love you!" Hearing those words for the first time from a boy Amanda's heart skipped a beat and she just melted as she looked back at him. She desperately wanted to say those same words to him but for some reason they seemed to stick in her throat. They experienced the passion of first love, but there was no sexual intimacy. She was always grateful for that. In later years, she wondered if they had experienced a sexual union, would it have made a difference in the way things turned out. He gave her, his class ring, his senior picture and wrote a beautiful and sentimental poem on it; one that she has never forgotten.

"But when the pain is too hard to bear,
Remember, Darling I'll be there,
To hold your hand and be your friend
Beyond the Stars, at journey's end."

These heartfelt words and moments have remained embedded in her memory.

Innocent and very romantic in her young years she thought it would last forever. Nevertheless, after dating for about eight months, something happened that always puzzled her all through the years. They slowly seemed to drift apart, and then it was over. She was saddened and lonesome for him for months after that. Perhaps the reason it did not last was the lack of sex, but Amanda never forgot the feeling she had for him, which so often happens with first love, and she never totally forgot him.

They spoke often of philosophical things, and he was the very first person to open Amanda's eyes to a different way of thinking from what she learned in her own home. She did not think too much about it at the time, but that awakening was the very beginning of what would lead to a life-long search for truth, wisdom and the meaning of life.

Having fun and enjoying all those years she graduated and secured a wonderful position with a financial company on the mainland; thoughts of Danny became just a lovely memory, but they never vanished completely, and neither did her love of singing and the theatre. For reasons unknown to her, life seemed to be taking her in a direction far away from those dreams.

Working for a wonderful man, she matured, gained a great deal of experience, and in time became his Executive Assistant. He was very good to her the five years she was with him. They went to lunch, dinner and sometimes dancing after the workday had ended. They celebrated Amanda's 21st birthday at a special restaurant called

"The 21", and he escorted her home in a chauffeured car. Rumors circulated around the office that they were involved in a love affair, but it was not true. He was her father's age and they were just employer and employee with a great fondness for each other.

She dated a couple of the company sales reps that came to town and spent a lot of time going to the theater and the opera. Always out in the evenings with an active social life she met many young men, but most often remained aloof. She was never easily attracted to anyone in particular the way she had been to Danny.

During one long hot summer, a new young man moved to the island. They met at a local pub and Amanda immediately knew he was quite taken with her. Bradley Moore constantly pursued her whenever they ran into each other. She eventually broke down and accepted a date. They continued to date often. She liked him a lot, but it did not quite feel like being in-love. They dated on and off for about a year and half. In that time her mother often reminded her of how he tended to drink a little too much. She also knew that all their friends drank too much. Therefore, she did not seem to be too concerned about it. Nevertheless, when she considered her mother's concern and the fact that he was more serious, she broke it off. As an independent, working woman, she was not remotely interested in the idea of marriage and children, but then something suddenly changed. After a couple of months being apart, she began to realize how much she missed Bradley. They had, after all become good friends. A few months later, after they resumed their dating relationship, something changed. Following an evening out while sitting in the car, they became extremely affectionate to each other. Suddenly, caught up in a moment of passion, they became intimate, which changed everything. She was just at the right stage to succumb to raging hormones, and a young woman's notions about falling in love. It did not help that Bradley's lovemaking was seductive and addicting. That moment catapulted them into a passionate and intense love affair. In later years, as Amanda matured and reminisced about their relationship, she often thought that it might have been more about raging hormones rather than anything else. Sometimes those hormones can cloud one's good judgment. Her gut feelings about the drinking should have been a red flag. However, there is always a reason for everything and the universe had something important in mind for this union, and Amanda's future.

Chapter 26

Mary

Mary and Aunt Iris were always busy with the activities at the church. One day while they were out Elizabeth received a phone call from Aunt Iris. Her words at the other end of the phone sounded as if she was upset and shaking. Elizabeth immediately became concerned. "What's wrong Aunt Iris?"

"Your mother has taken a fall on the steps of the church. They are taking her to the hospital. Please meet us there."

Elizabeth grabbed her purse and the keys to the car, and was out the door in a flash. Everyone else was working.

When Elizabeth arrived at the hospital Aunt Iris was in the waiting room. She told Elizabeth that her mother was in surgery since she had broken her hip in the fall. They waited for several hours before the doctor came to talk to them. Studying the expression on his face as he came down the hall, she had a premonition of what he was going to say. Mary had not survived the surgery. Aunt Iris now eighty-nine stumbled as she hurried to get up in order to hear what they were discussing. Elizabeth put her arms around her tightly and comforted her as she learned the news. They had been loving sisters and companions since William's passing. Preparations for her funeral began as they arrived home. Mary would now rest beside her beloved husband William, in the same churchyard with Harry, Jane, Alice and little Tommy.

Elizabeth was distraught and depressed as she dealt with her mother's death. She was also very concerned about Aunt Iris. However, as the days after the funeral moved them further from the passing of their loved one they surged forward and back into the mainstream of life. The passage of time is always healing.

Aunt Iris settled into a life without her beloved sister. She was definitely a survivor and had a strong constitution. Everyone in the family knew that!

Chapter 27

Amanda and Bradley

Mary left a small inheritance to Elizabeth and that would certainly benefit the family in the days to come. Shortly after Mary's passing, Amanda and Bradley announced their engagement. The money left to Elizabeth would help to pay for a lovely wedding for Amanda.

Learning from Amanda about her engagement, Amanda's boss invited them both to dinner to celebrate. It was a pleasant evening with good conversation and food. After meeting Bradley and spending the evening with them, he seemed to have some concerns about their relationship. The next day at work Charles Draper took Amanda aside and said to her, "Your guy, Bradley, he is not the man for you!" Amanda was shocked. Nevertheless, she seemed to feel that now she *was* really in love, and six months later in the fall of 1963, she and Bradley Moore were married. Charles' words would resurface many times in years to come. In the final analysis, he would turn out to be right. However, if it were not for their marriage, Amanda would not have the great joy of having a wonderful daughter. Moreover, that made up for any negativity that had been part of their marriage. Sometimes dreams must be put on hold until a future date for reasons unknown to us at the time. The Universe, Source Energy, or God some might say, works in mysterious ways that we do not understand.

Bradley was the second person in Amanda's life to add to her growth and enlightenment in the areas of religion, science and philosophy. He was an avowed agnostic and wanted a simple life. Having studied Zen Buddhism he enlightened her with ideas he had learned and she ultimately moved from the limited thinking of her upbringing to a more liberal and open-minded philosophical outlook on life. She completely let go of any belief in the dogma and doctrine of Catholicism. Nevertheless, her traditional upbringing was still influencing many of her choices. She desired a good provider, a lovely home and all the trimmings. They had many discussions on these topics throughout their years together. The agreed on some things and disagreed on others, but the philosophical ideas they shared and discussed were an inspiring part of their relationship. However, Bradley's drinking issue continued to be a problem. It always made its presence known, in so many areas of their lives, mostly at an inappropriate moment. Even though their intimate life seemed the best part of their relationship and through the years Amanda had grown to love Bradley dearly, she struggled with his behavior.

The universe always has reasons for directing ones future, which is why it is sometimes best to "go with the flow" rather than try to control outcomes. Amanda attempted to go with the flow for several years, always hoping something would change.

Within the first two years Amanda gave birth to an adorable little girl, they named Victoria. They lived in a small town, their daily lives just like most young couples starting out in life. He went to work; she stayed home and cared for Victoria, cooked meals and spent a lot of time decorating their home. Victoria was a model child. A beautiful little girl she was very well behaved and a wonderful joy in Amanda's life. Even so, as Victoria grew Amanda became fidgety and wanted something more outside the home. Her Dad, Jack Cole had his own consulting business with a partner and offered his daughter a part time job. Elizabeth jumped at the chance to care for her first grandchild a couple of days a week. For the time being Amanda seemed content, but it did not last. As the years passed and Victoria was in school, Amanda continued to feel that there was something missing in her life, but not exactly sure just what it was. Fate was beginning to play its hand and was knocking at Amanda's door.

An opportunity came along for her to go into real estate and she jumped at the opportunity. She did well, seemed satisfied and it provided her with her own income for several years.

One evening the phone rang. It was Elizabeth calling to let Amanda and Bradley know that Aunt Iris had quietly passed away in her sleep. She was ninety-eight. Her life was long, ambitious, healthy and certainly gutsy. She had been an inspiration to everyone, especially to Amanda, and the family would miss her presence. After the funeral and a period of grieving, their lives returned to normal.

Amanda's temporary satisfaction soon seemed to dissipate and her feelings of discontent rapidly resurfaced, even though she had grown to love Bradley, dearly. She sensed the same discontent in Bradley. They experienced so many major differences in the way they wanted to conduct their lives. Victoria was becoming a young woman and her graduation from high school was imminent. Bradley loved the cold winters of north. Thoughts of having to live through another one sent a chill up Amanda's spine. She had always dreamed of living in Florida. And, something deep inside along with her dreams, was once again knocking, and inspiring her to make a major life-change. Bradley's drinking became a constant source of irritation. Daily levels of frustration caused by their differences continuously left her in a state of discontent. After hours of soul searching and many, many discussions, and the fact that they were approaching mid-life, Bradley and Amanda began to discover that they had been slowly growing apart. They always had different goals and interests. There were many difficulties, through the years. Marriage, in Amanda's mind, had not turned out to be what she had thought it *would* be. Although, she was not really sure what she thought it *should* be. All through the years, she longed for a peace within, and that intuitive voice inside knew that seemed unreachable if she stayed in the marriage.

That disappointment, her childhood dreams and her search for peace and contentment enabled her to decide that she wanted to be on her own, and do what was in the deepest corner of her heart. The drinking issue was just one more major reason to help her in moving forward to her future. After many late nights of just sitting and thinking, she began to realize that the music, singing and dancing that had been such a part of her years growing up had been missing now for quite a while. Due to her many philosophical studies and an insatiable desire for more knowledge in that area, elevated her inclination to move forward on her path. She often wondered what had given her such a longing for life's meaning, accompanied by a feeling of independence and autonomy. She was ready to approach the future without any fear of starting in a new direction at mid-life.

It was not long before she began to realize that her experience of three months in the hospital as a young child of seven, isolated from her parents, had provided her with that strength. Now she was beginning to understand that experience had given her one of life's greatest gifts. She awakened to the fact that it was directing her decision to completely change her life, and begin a new chapter. Tugging at her heart, was her insatiable love of music, a desire to sing and an unquenchable thirst for wisdom. A secret dream of living in Florida inspired her decision to take a trip to visit a friend there. She intuitively knew the only way she was going to achieve her dreams was to make this change. This was going to be her adventure.

Joyce, a long-time friend from previous years, was working for a manufacturing company there. Amanda decided to call her. After some initial conversation and the real reason for her call, Joyce told her there were some job openings at her company. "If you have any interest, I encourage you to make a trip to Florida for an interview. "You can stay with me and we can share some time together as well." After much consideration, Amanda booked a flight. Bradley was amiable to her decision.

The interview went extremely well. Joyce and Amanda spent some quality moments rehashing old times. A couple of days passed and the phone rang. It was for Amanda. Joyce already knew what the person on the other end of the phone was about to say. Amanda's happy smiling face disclosed to her friend that she would soon be living in Florida.

Memories of her feelings for Danny were a constant reminder of some of the things that had been missing in her marriage. Growing old with regrets, or leaving this world with her music and dreams buried somewhere inside were not going to be the way her life would play out! Never seeking fame as her goal at this stage of her life, she just dreamed of the fun and enjoyment of singing to a live audience, as well as participating in some form of dancing.

Upon her return from Florida, Bradley did not oppose her decision and they agreed to a mutual parting. Victoria, now heading for college, left Amanda free to follow those dreams. Her other life-long desire of moving to Florida was where, in her heart, she knew might be the place to see all her dreams come to fruition.

The house seemed empty with Victoria gone off to school. Alone now, she and Bradley were making plans to separate and each make a life of their own. She began to pack for the move. Bradley agreed to help her with the physical move. Respecting each other's choices, they intuitively seemed to know that this was the best decision for them both.

Chapter 28

Manifesting A Special Dream

Her memory of Danny kept surfacing, and her curiosity of where he was and what his life was like always remained in the back of her mind.

Before making her final move to Florida, she planned a vacation to Cape Cod with her girlfriend, Jeannette who lived in New York. They met at the airport in Boston and rented a car. A lovely waterfront condo awaited their arrival. They took in all the sights. During a ferry ride to Martha's Vineyard, she noticed a man staring at her from the other side of the ferry. When she glanced his way, he quickly re-focused his attention to the woman at his side. Amanda gazed at him for some time without his knowledge. When she looked a little closer, her heart skipped a beat and a burst of emotion welled up inside her as she realized it was Danny. The years had changed him but not enough that she did not recognize his handsome face, his beautiful wavy hair, now streaked with gray and his kind and gentle eyes. She had always known that he lived somewhere in the Massachusetts area. Excited, her first impulse was to run over and say hello but she held herself back. Since he was with someone unknown to her, she wondered if it might be inappropriate and, besides, she was not at all sure she would be able to keep her composure.

As the ferry was docking someone suddenly tapped her on the shoulder, "Amanda, is it you?"

Her heart beating faster now, she turned and looked into his eyes, "Yes, Danny, I thought that was you over there but I wasn't positive." "It's been a long time… about 30 years, I think. I never thought I would ever see you again, although I had always hoped. I noticed that you were standing with a lovely lady." "Yes, Amanda, that is my wife. She went to sit in the car since we are almost at the dock." "That's a shame I would have loved to meet her." "That might have been awkward since I have never told her about us. Well, the ferry is docking so I must go. It was wonderful to see you again." He leaned over and hugged her gently and then he was gone. She was shaking. At that moment, she knew what she had always suspected…that she had never gotten over him completely, and wondered if he felt the same. Suddenly, Jeanette was at her side, "Who was that?" "Oh, just someone I knew a long time ago."

They thoroughly enjoyed their trip to Cape Cod. However, Jeanette's curiosity about Amanda's encounter on the ferry was literally driving her nuts.

A couple of weeks after their return during a phone conversation, Jeanette insisted that Amanda tell her what took place in that meeting with Danny. Without going into all the details, she gave Jeanette a synopsis of her relationship with Danny in high school. As they continued their conversation, Jeanette shared a story about her high school sweetheart. So they found common ground and understanding in similar experiences from their past. Whenever they spent time together, they spoke about Danny and the idea of a possible reunion. Jeanette continuously encouraged her to pursue it and Amanda always wondered if it might become a reality one day.

All through the years, Amanda had always wished for a sister or a close girlfriend. As it has turned out Jeanette had become that girlfriend.

When Bradley was busy with his work life Amanda found ways to keep herself occupied whenever she did not have a part time job. She volunteered with organizations and began to meet many new friends. At one event, she met Jeanette. They seemed to have an instant connection. Not long after that, they were spending lots of time together, shopping, having lunch with other women and playing Mah Jongg.

When Jeanette was in the throws of a divorce and was soon to begin a new career, Amanda offered to take care of her four-year-old son temporarily. Fast-forwarding a couple of years, Jeanette met a man, they dated for about a year and in time; they planned to be married. She asked Amanda to be the maid of honor. Through the years, often separated by miles, they continued to nurture and enjoy a wonderful friendship. They visited each other often whenever possible.

Chapter 29

1984 - 89 Early Florida Years

Amanda manifested her dream and settled into a life in Florida while Victoria became accustomed to college life. Finding herself in a new place without any friends, her new neighbor gives her a small local newspaper. Thumbing through the pages searching for things to do, she peruses the classified section. As if by some magic, or someone listening to the longings of her heart, one ad in bold print that reads *VOICE INSTRUCTION* seems to jump off the page. Because of a lifelong dream to sing, her heart flutters for a moment and she decides to call. A woman's voice answers, "Nichols vocal studio". Amanda introduces herself, asks for information and offers some background about her desire to sing. Joan Nichols suggests a first lesson and an evaluation without any cost. During their conversation, she notices that Amanda seems hesitant to accept for whatever reason. Joan emphatically tells her, "Amanda, if you do not take this opportunity you will always be sorry." Convinced, she sets up the first appointment. That was the beginning.

Busy with a hectic career in inside sales, Amanda studied voice, with this special vocal teacher and coach over a period of three years. In time, she was doing singing engagements. After several months of private and group ballroom dance lessons, she became quite proficient. Occasionally, she did a ballroom show with a dance partner and entered competitions with her dance teacher. At the same time, she was building a new mid-life career. Constantly in her mind was the memory of that brief meeting with Danny on the ferry. She could not let it go.

As she moved through her workday, there was always something to look forward to at the close of business: a voice lesson, a ballroom dance or an evening out with friends. A variety of interesting encounters began to show up in her social life. On one occasion while out with Joyce and some business colleagues an extremely handsome young man joined the group. During the introduction, their eyes met and something happened that they both felt. If it had been dark enough at the time, the group might have witnessed some sort of light show. The energy sparks that flew between them might have lighted the entire room. It seemed like he deliberately sat at the opposite end of the table. By the end of the evening, as most of the group had gone home and there were only three of them left, he was at Amanda's side.

After a short time Joyce, Amanda's friend and work colleague, got up and announced it was getting late and she was heading for home. That left the two of them alone. They talked for a little while and she was surprised to learn he was an outside sales rep for the same company. Prior to that evening, they had never met. The place was emptying and Frank Toomey, as he had been introduced, suggested that they might go to another spot that had music, and was open until the wee hours. They could have a nightcap and dance a little. Amanda agreed. *Wow dancing, a guy after my own heart.* she thought. They drove their own cars to a nightclub a few miles away. Driving through the empty streets rather late on a weeknight, Amanda's mind was racing with all kinds of thoughts about where this new adventure might take her. Dancing with Frank in a dark nightclub atmosphere might prove to be dangerous, judging from what took place when they first met. She was ready for whatever the rest of the night presented. She did wonder how old he was since he appeared to be quite a bit younger than she was at this stage of her life. As it turned out, he was…about twenty years younger, with gorgeous dark brown wavy hair and a beautifully well-tanned, and well-toned body. She still looked great at forty-five so he probably could not tell her age. She had kept her figure well, had long dark brown curly hair and a golden tan.

They met at the door to the nightclub. Frank took charge and asked for a table near the dance-floor. As they sat down the waiter was there to take their order. They ordered a couple of drinks and chatted a bit while the band was on a break. When the music resumed Frank offered her his hand and gave her an eye-signal that told her he wanted to dance. Up on her feet in a split second he led her to the dance-floor. The music was slow and romantic. They both felt a strong attraction and they moved slowly and deliberately closer. Her heart was pounding and she thought, *I think we are heading into dangerous water here, but I am going for it.* They moved to the music and then he suddenly pulled away slightly, looked down at her and gently kissed her.

As the music ended they sat down and resumed talking, telling each other about their private lives. He was in the throes of a divorce and thinking of leaving the company to go to the competition. She was new to the company so she was surprised. If he accepted the new job, it would take him across the state of Florida to the west coast.

It was not long before he, once again, was leading her to the dance-floor. That first kiss behind them their attraction to each other was increasing, and the passion was heightened. After several dances, Amanda whispered in his ear, "Let's get out of here and go to my apartment." He did not object.

She unlocked and opened the door. He followed her and closed the door behind them. He eagerly embraced her and their lips met again. As they deliberately moved to the bedroom, they left a trail of their clothing on the floor. All at once, they were rolling around on the bed and then suddenly they were making love, since all their foreplay had taken place on the dance-floor. When the ecstasy subsided, they lay there in each other's arms. They talked until dawn.

Rising and dashing madly to shower they dressed and headed to the office where Frank had an early meeting. Having no time to spare, they dressed in the same clothes. Amanda arrived a little later and started her day with excitement wondering about this new experience.

A couple of days later her colleague, Joyce made some sarcastic comments about the fact that both she and Frank were wearing the same clothes to work the day after they were all out together. She quizzed Amanda about their encounter, which Amanda was saved from answering by the ringing of her phone. It was Frank calling her from the road. He asked her to have dinner with him on Saturday evening, to which she immediately accepted. Excited and enthusiastic it seemed to take forever for Saturday night to arrive.

Saturday showed up and the doorbell rang. As she opened the door, he swept her up in his arms, twirled her around and said, "You look gorgeous!" She was all golden tan with her long dark brown curly hair hanging to her shoulders. A fitted raspberry sleeveless, crocheted top accented her waist and hugged her hips over a short white linen skirt. As she caught a glimpse of herself in the mirror she thought, "Yes, I do look gorgeous." He apologized for not being as dressed up as she was. However, he looked great to her, dark hair and a beautiful Florida tan, his perfectly pressed light blue denims, caramel loafers (no socks), an expertly pressed, pink button down collar Polo shirt that made him look "scrumptious"!

They dined and danced at a local hot spot. Dinner finished, they drove to the beach and sat in the car watching the moon shining over the ocean. He put his arm around her, drew her to him and kissed her gently. "Let's go back to your place, I need to talk to you but I really want to ravish you."

Once again, they wasted no time getting to the bedroom. When their lovemaking ended, he suddenly became serious. "I have accepted that new job offer and they want me on the west coast ASAP. I will be leaving tomorrow. I am so sorry that this will have to end when it was just beginning." "I understand, Frank, but I enjoyed every minute of the time we spent together." He stayed the night and left at daybreak. They saw each other briefly in the office the next day and said good-bye in the parking lot. He was gone out of her life as quickly as he had come into it. Truthfully, it would not have gone anywhere due to the difference in their ages. Eventually he would have been looking for a new young wife. It had been lovely, but better left a fond memory. It was a once in a lifetime, romantic encounter with a much younger man that would be remembered always.

Following Frank's departure from the company Amanda became an executive assistant to the vice president of operations. Philip Taylor was an exceptional superior and she loved working for him. Also in charge of the engineering department, he trusted Amanda with a number of vital engineering projects. When it was time to build a new manufacturing plant, he put her in charge of all the administrative work. She became a liaison between him and all the contractors. Her workdays were inspiring and productive for the next several years while they finished the construction of the new facility.

As time passed, the company was acquired by a much larger one. The sitting president was about to be replaced with someone new. Amanda quickly learned how different a new corporate culture could be under new leadership. The first directive to employees was, "*We operate lean and mean!*" Implementing many changes, the new management also discharged several employees. Retention and reassignment to a new position was a relief for Amanda. Heading up the regional human resources department without any prior experience in that area, became a challenge, especially having to report to a new manager. Forging ahead with great determination, she excelled. However, losing so many employees doubled everyone's workload. Her life beyond her workday soon became a respite from the stresses of each new day. Inspiration about her career, and her eagerness to begin each new day was rapidly waning.

Ballroom dancing to the wee hours always brought Amanda great joy. One evening feeling wonderful as she was driving home, attempting to enter a major four-lane highway, she almost hit the rear end of the car in front of her, when the driver suddenly stopped. Stomping on the breaks and swerving to miss the other car's bumper, her car skidded and quickly moved on to the highway and did a 180 degree turn across all four lanes. In a panic, she observed all the lights of the cars moving toward her as she checked her rear-view mirror. It all happened so quickly and suddenly she was against the center guardrail facing the wrong direction. Her heart pounding, as she tried to regain her composure, she wondered what just happened. As her state of consciousness returned to the present moment, she quickly realized that this could have been a tragedy for her and many others. She immediately felt grateful for her safety. In that instant, she intuitively felt that she and the on-coming traffic had been suspended in a moment when time stopped, to keep her safe. There seemed to be no other explanation. She had things to do, more lessons to learn and more life to live...it just was not her time. What could have been a terrible life-threatening accident was held in abeyance for whatever reason. Was it fate or destiny playing its hand? The incident puzzled her for months. It was in that very moment in time Amanda discovered a strong faith in a force greater than herself, which is also within each one of us. Continuing to return to the same conclusion, that still small voice in her head kept whispering that, perhaps, there was something better coming in her future, and she needed to stick around.

Chapter 30

Family Update

Amanda was thrilled to learn from Jack Jr. that their parents had decided to move to Florida to be near the children and grandkids. Never married, Ted had always remained in his parent's home and assisted them, as they got older. He was coming with them. Now they could see each other more often and spend the holidays all together.

Jack, Jr now living in Florida for a few years, was married for the second time, and busy raising his children, all currently in their teenage years. This was a quite challenge at times for both him and his new wife.

Elizabeth and Jack were aging. Jack's sister Anne, who had been their maid of honor, was now close to ninety and still in good health, but alone. So, she moved in with them. Jack was slowly becoming somewhat sedentary but Elizabeth remained active. She and Ted bowled once a week and she was involved in the activities of the local Catholic Church. Their daily life seemed quiet, peaceful and uneventful.

Chapter 31

1989 - 1990 A Special Love

Spending leisurely Sunday afternoons at Tea Dances at a beautiful local hotel, Amanda would meet several folks she knew from the dance world. One memorable Sunday when she entered the ballroom with tables filled, she searched for a place to sit. Someone she knew waved her over to her table. "Come sit with us, we have an extra chair." Just then, the music began and everyone selected a partner and went to the dance-floor. Sitting alone, she glanced at the next table and saw a man alone. Looking away quickly she thought, *"I am going to ask him to dance."* As she turned to get up, he was there in front of her. "Would you like to dance?" "I would love to," she replied. Their first dance was a waltz. The song was, *Can I Have This Dance for the Rest of My Life*. At that moment, she had absolutely no knowledge of the significance that song would have one day.

At the band's next break, a raffle was held and Rudy Schultz won breakfast for two for the brunch the following Sunday. He invited Amanda. Even though she really did not know him, he was so delightful that she accepted immediately. That next week seemed to pass by so slowly and finally Sunday arrived. She was excited and was anxious to learn more about the lovely man who had just come into her life.

Brunch was wonderful and so was their conversation. They exchanged information about each other and when it was time to leave, he asked her for another date. That was the beginning. During their first month, they spent a lot of time together. He stayed a couple of weekends at her new villa; they went dancing and shared many intimate moments. They seemed to settle into a comfortable relationship very quickly. At their first month anniversary, Rudy showed up with a lovely card to celebrate their time together. Inside the card were airline tickets to Hawaii. Amanda was in shock but absolutely delighted. She hugged and kissed him with a grateful heart. The next day they spent the entire day in bed. In the weeks prior to the trip Amanda often thought, "*I am going to a place thousands of miles away, with a man I hardly know...but it just seems so right.*"

As they waited for the trip to Hawaii to arrive, they took dance classes together and Rudy moved some of his things into her home so they could be together on a more regular basis. Hawaii was beckoning and in no time, they were off on a beautiful trip, returning ten days later. Not much time passed and one of the dance studios that they frequented was sponsoring a dance cruise to the Caribbean. Rudy decided that they should go, and Amanda was delighted, but beginning to feel like they were on a roller coaster ride.

Returning from the cruise their life became routine. Rudy mentioned marriage, but that was entirely too fast for Amanda. It had only been a few months since they started dating. *"You are moving a little too fast for me, so, let's put that idea on hold, at least temporarily,"* Amanda responded.

With the holidays, fast approaching Rudy came up with another surprise…a New Year's Eve Cruise. A family Christmas came and went and they were off on another adventure to the Caribbean. When they returned, there was a message from his daughter that she planned to be married in the spring. This meant a trip to New Jersey for the wedding. Everything seemed to be moving so quickly!

Following the wedding they, once again, settled back into their routine for a few months. The summer almost over, Rudy and his insatiable longing to travel, decided that they might take a trip to California in the fall and drive the coastal highway. He made all the reservations and when September rolled around, they were busy with preparations for that trip. Landing in L.A. a week later, Rudy rented a convertible for the trip up the Pacific Coast Highway. They stopped all along the way to enjoy the breathtaking views and stayed in charming Bed and Breakfast Inns. Amanda's favorite place was Carmel where they toured the city, had a couple of lovely dinners, watched a sunset on Carmel Beach and spent several romantic evenings sipping Champaign, in a room with a cozy fireplace. Enjoying a trip to Yosemite National Park and relishing in its majestic beauty, they spent the next full day and night in San Francisco, prior to the flight home.

The night before they were to leave, they undressed and settled into bed. When Amanda moved close to Rudy, she became alarmed as to how hot his body felt. He seemed to be running a high fever, but he never mentioned not feeling well, as they toured San Francisco. She was worried, why should he have such a high fever? He told her not to be such a worrywart that he would be just fine, and they drifted off to sleep.

Hurrying to catch their plane through the busy airport they arrived at the gate just in time, took their seats and they were on their way back home.

On the first day home Amanda insisted Rudy go to the doctor immediately. When he returned the Dr.'s diagnosis was a respiratory infection and he prescribed an antibiotic. Things seemed to return to normal. Entering a dance contest before the trip, they competed two days after returning from California. At the end of the competition, the announcer named them as the first place winners. Before beginning the drive home, they sat in the car and admired a shiny new trophy, feeling very proud of their dancing.

Two days later, Amanda was waiting for Rudy to return from an aerobics class. It was about 9:00 PM when he came through the door. He said he was very tired and was going to take a shower and go to bed. Amanda got into bed and waited for him to join her. He slipped in next to her and she turned out the lights. Not two minutes later, he made a very odd noise. She thought he was kidding, as he always loved teasing her. She spoke to him but he did not answer. She turned on the light, looked at him and her heart started to pound. His eyes were rolled back in his head and he wasn't breathing. She jumped out of bed, dialed 911 and then tried to administer CPR without success. It seemed like the paramedics were taking forever. She looked at him again and now his color was grey. She ran into the street as she heard the sirens in order to direct them to her home. They asked her if he was alive…she responded, "I don't think so." They tried to revive him and then moved him to the ambulance to go to the hospital. Amanda rode in the ambulance with him. He was taken in immediately and she went to the waiting room. Then the doctor called her in to another room to talk to her. She already knew what he was going to tell her.

That was the most lonely, traumatic night of Amanda's life as she stayed up most of the night lying on the sofa. It was much too difficult to return to the bed where he had passed out of her life in the blink of an eye. They had enjoyed a wonderful fifteen months together but now it was over. It was no wonder that their relationship moved forward so quickly. It was clear to her that the song that played for their first dance would always be remembered because his sudden death gave it so much meaning. Being blessed with the support and love of family and friends, she was comforted in her grief.

The next few months she tried to adjust to life without him. It was difficult. She felt like someone had punched her in the stomach. She grieved, but she had great inner strength and as time passed, she gradually returned to her single life, as it had been before their relationship.

Amanda was beginning to understand how life could change in an instant. This single moment in her life had changed her. She had grown wiser and more empathetic.

She learned about vulnerability. He had taught her about love in a way that she had not fully experienced, prior to their relationship. The universe once again, had given her a great gift, and a magnificent lesson. Enjoy each moment of life as they come, because nothing lasts forever…except the love that one experiences.

That year, as Thanksgiving approached, Jeanette aware of the sadness in Amanda's life, invited she and Victoria to New York, where Jeanette was now living in the Hamptons.

It was a great trip and Amanda so enjoyed her reconnection with Jeanette. Grateful for a beautiful friendship Amanda assured Jeanette they would talk often on the phone, and visit whenever time permitted.

Chapter 32

New Insight - 1991

Witnessing the sudden death of a man she loved and the immediate loneliness of such a life event became a great awakening. It became the impetus for her as she continued to delve into her metaphysical, spiritual and philosophical studies.

An opportunity to do a workshop with a new author and speaker, Maryanne Williamson at the Esalen Institute in Big Sur, California fell into Amanda's lap, so to speak. A wonderful friend and mentor, Barbara was given a scholarship to the workshop by Maryanne after meeting her at a book signing. Barbara did not want to travel alone so she invited Amanda join her. Eugene, Oregon was their first stop where they toured the city and spent a day with friends in the country. Next stop would be LA and a ride up the coastal highway. They ultimately planned a two-week trip around the workshop, and visited many sites of some of the great metaphysical teacher's of the past, and new thought teachers of the present. They drove the coast highway from LA to San Francisco with many stops along the way. Travelling back to L.A., they experienced a fabulous train ride and the splendor of picturesque views of the ocean and landscape. They encountered many interesting people, and some fascinating characters along the way. It turned out to be a once in a lifetime trip.

Returning they learned that an organization known as The Institute of Noetic Sciences (IONS) was doing their annual conference in Boca Raton where they both lived. Another new door was about to open for Amanda. She attended the conference on a scholarship and was able to participate in so many wonderful workshops with many more of the new thought leaders that were springing up everywhere. She learned about Edgar Mitchell, Apollo 14 astronaut, one of twelve men who had walked on the moon. He was the founder of IONS, and his experience on his way back from the moon led him to create that organization. She had the great pleasure of meeting him and his family. This was just the beginning of Amanda's association with that organization.

Good fortune and new philosophical insights were appearing everywhere she turned, and continued to knock at her door and enlighten her. Studying all the great inspirational and metaphysical leaders of yesterday and today, she was quickly moving forward on her path of personal growth and knowledge.

Becoming a serious student of the many philosophies that were presenting themselves, she began a daily practice of meditation. Initially, she found it difficult to quiet her internal dialogue. With time and determination as the roof-brain chatter began to dissipate, she surrounded herself with a protective white light. In a deeply spiritual meditative moment of complete silence and feeling disconnected from her body without any physical sensation, something happened she was not prepared for. In her mind's eye, was nothing but an ocean of blue light. Blissful feelings of total peace enveloped her. Remaining there for some time, she did not want to return to her normal state of being. But, then suddenly as a thought edged its way in, she returned to a natural state of awareness. For several minutes, she just sat and relished in the residual of the experience. The more she pondered it, she began to realize that this must be what death is like. It truly felt like dying while you are still alive. She was never able to repeat the exact experience but the blissful feelings and a sense of total peace have remained. The most significant result was a complete release in any fear of death.

Chapter 33
1991 - 1995 Family Update

As Jack and Elizabeth moved into their golden years, Jack's lack of mobility caused him to become very unsteady on his feet, which eventually resulted in a broke hip. Hospitalized he was prepared for surgery. Elizabeth had great hopes that he would recover and become active once again. When the doctor delivered the shocking news he had not survived the surgery, she was devastated since they had just celebrated their 50th wedding anniversary. Amanda was out of town at the time but the boys were there to support their Mom in this time of loss for all of them.

After Jack passed, his sister Ann chose to enter a senior living facility where she remained for the next several years. Ted was his mother's constant companion and assisted her with everything in the home. Elizabeth did not fair well after Jack's death. She became lethargic and uninterested in life. After years of smoking, her breathing so labored, she could not move around without the aid of oxygen. Like her father, whose breath was restricted due to smoke inhalation from years of fighting fires. Both Elizabeth and her father William spent their final years, shortly before their passing, wearing oxygen masks, confined to sitting on a sofa.

For the next couple of years she rarely left the house, or the sofa. Then one day noticing her lack of breathing as she sat in her chair, Ted could not revive her and called the paramedics. Amanda was at work and so was Jack. Ted called and asked them to meet him at the hospital. When they arrived, they learned that Elizabeth had already passed away. Only days before, due to her inability to breathe, she had told Ted that she wished she would die. Amanda, Ted and Jack were all in shock at the loss of their dear mother. As the devastation subsided after the funeral, they realized that they all felt relieved because without her struggle to breathe, she would be able to rest peacefully.

As the grief began to lessen, they all returned to their daily lives. Jack, Jr. divorced his second wife and not much time had passed when he took another walk down the aisle. His kids were still troublesome. Aunt Anne, who was about to turn ninety-five, was now the only surviving senior member of the family. Jack Jr. was in charge of handling her affairs. Moving her to a senior living facility, he and his wife visited her often, and so did Amanda when time permitted.

During one visit to see Aunt Anne, Amanda realized just how much time she spent just going within herself. Her severely impaired hearing and eyesight kept her from listening or watching TV. She had always been a great reader, but unfortunately, those days were behind her. Being a devout Catholic she spent a great deal of her time in reflection and contemplation. In one conversation, Amanda learned how Aunt Anne had come to know that there are no coincidences and that fate, a creative force,

God, or the universe play a huge role in life. She expressed to Amanda how she now knew that everything is planned. Using as an example she told Amanda, "I absolutely now understand that your mother and father were meant to meet as they did, and have you and the boys." Amanda was taken back hearing this statement. Because of her own spiritual studies, she knew at that moment that Aunt Anne's long spiritual life and her devotion to her beliefs had given her great insight and wisdom. Now, nearing the end of life she was able to express this inner knowing.

Shortly after Amanda's visit, Jack, Jr. gave her a party at his home for her ninety-fifth birthday. Amanda and Ted attended. Several weeks later Jack received a call from the senior living center. Aunt Anne was in the hospital. It did not seem to be anything too serious but she was beginning to fail. The next evening, they all went to the hospital to see her. She was alert and pleased to see them. Several hours later as Jack was trying to rest, the phone rang. It was the hospital calling to say that she had passed peacefully in her sleep. Now, she too was gone after ninety-five long years. Amanda, Ted and Jack Jr., who were once the new generation, were now the senior members of the family.

With the passing of Elizabeth, Ted remained alone and eventually entered a senior living facility in central Florida. Jack Jr. divorced for the third time and finally seemed content, living the single life a short distance from his children, grandchildren and Ted.

Time rushes by and life keeps changing occasionally with tears, most often with joy, but always moving forward.

Chapter 34

1995 - 1996 New Horizons for Amanda

As Amanda continued to readjust to her single life she was engaged with her career, singing and dancing the nights away where the sky is almost always azure blue, the water deep aqua and the tropical foliage lush and green...a paradise to Amanda...she was content living in her favorite place.

As her love of singing continued, she became a frequent soloist at the local Science of Mind Sunday service, and at an occasional wedding. She managed to book shows at a few of the local condo communities. At a nearby piano bar and restaurant, where she spent weekend evenings through the years, the piano player always invited her to sing a set.

Her love affair with metaphysics, and the role of consciousness and spirituality grew exponentially as she attended more workshops with wonderful inspirational speakers such as Wayne Dyer, Deepak Chopra, Louise Hay, Brian Weiss and so many others. She reads as many books as she can get her hands on.

Reading a book by Wayne Dyer, she learned about his quote, *"Don't die with your music inside"*. That statement validated her feelings and the decision she made to take a risk and manifest the longings of her heart. She was so grateful for all his wisdom. She now knew that what he wrote about was all-true, because she was living that truth.

The years seemed to disappear. Her career position of twelve years was beginning to cause unending stress. Working demands became intolerable and the company atmosphere was very toxic. Attending a final staff meeting in California she returned knowing she was going to resign. She intuitively knew that kind of atmosphere would have long-term negative effects on her physical and mental health. Not willing to jeopardize her future, and with a feeling of dread as she faced each new day, she knew in her heart that the only way she would maintain a quality life would be to leave, and move on. The negative influence of her work environment played havoc with the inner peace she so treasured, and chose to maintain. The still small voice within her quietly whispered *resigning will be your salvation*. Once again destiny, her intuition or the universe was calling her to move forward.

Just prior to her resignation, her boss called her from California requesting that she call and interview a sales rep that her company was trying to hire from the competition. Here comes fate and another serendipitous occasion showing up in her life. She listened as her boss utters the man's name…Frank Toomey. It has been ten years since their brief romantic encounter.

The next day Amanda called Frank and set up a lunch date. They agreed to meet at a local restaurant. As she stepped out of her car, he approached her and deliberately looked her up and down. "Wow, you still look fabulous, Amanda. Time has certainly treated you well." Graciously she thanked him and wanted to say the same thing but at first said nothing. She was busy noticing that he was no longer that young person with whom she had experienced a brief passionate affair. More mature in appearance and demeanor, he was one gorgeous hunk of a man. Then suddenly she blurted out, "You look better than ever."

They chatted for a while and brought each other up to date on their lives. She learned that he was now married for the second time. Then their conversation turned to business. He was aware of the reason for their lunch knowing she was currently in charge of the regional Human Resources department of his former employer. He made no bones about the fact that he did not intend to change his work life. His present company, knowing this meeting was to take place, had made him an offer he could not refuse. Amanda always knew that he was a professional "hotshot" salesperson that the company would not want to lose. Lunch completed, they say their goodbyes, concluding another brief moment in one's life, and they went their separate ways. It *was* fun and interesting seeing him after ten years, and reminiscing about their brief encounter.

When she returned to the office she submitted her resignation.

Chapter 35

1998-2000 - Victoria

While Amanda's work and social life continued to move rapidly forward, Victoria's did as well.

Victoria met Eddie Blake while they were both attending the same university. At first it was an on and off romance. Eventually, they both knew that they wanted to make a life together and they did for a number of years, with no marriage plans. While their careers were developing, they spent all their spare time together. When vacation time rolled around, they traveled all over Europe and visited many of the great ski resorts in the mountains of Colorado.

Managing a very successful sales career Victoria was offered a management position, and learned she was going to be transferred to North Carolina. Fortunately, Eddie was able to get a transfer within his company to the same area. As those events were unfolding, they were also beginning to plan a magical wedding at Walt Disney World in Orlando.

The wedding was magical. Amanda, outfitted in a black and white ensemble wore the broach that Jane left to her mother, Elizabeth. The same one Jane wore the day of William's marriage to Mary. A stunning bride, Victoria wore the lavalier that Mary had worn on the day of her marriage. She was a lovely vision in a full-length white satin gown, with a beautifully beaded strapless bodice, fitted at the waist.

Following all the festivities, they spent a weeklong honeymoon in Italy. Returning they settled into their new work positions, and moved into a new home. Not much time passed before Victoria announced that she was expecting. She continued to work until the end of her pregnancy.

Chapter 36

A Career Change

Just as independent, self-reliant and determined as her great grandmother Jane, Amanda resisted any fear, and was confident that the universe would open new doors for her. Later that week when she handed in her resignation her heart fluttered for a moment and she wondered what her future would be. A bold move on her part, since she was single, self-supporting and had no new position on the horizon. As a result of her philosophical, spiritual and metaphysical studies, she knew that fear would only block or hold up the process of a new beginning, so she remained in a positive state of mind. Income from a rental property was enough to hold her over for a while. Working temporary jobs to keep the money coming in, she never sent out one resume. Without any doubt, she trusted that something was waiting for her, and the universe presented it right on time. One of her temporary employers offered her a permanent spot as a Financial Administrator where the work environment was very busy, but the atmosphere congenial, harmonious and with very little stress. She remained happily employed there for the next several years. All through her life, she always felt protected as if someone or something somewhere was continuously guiding her life, and watching over her.

When her vacation time approached, she decided to take another trip to Cape Cod. Always in her mind and heart was the possibility of another encounter with Danny. This time she decided to go alone. Lingering in the back of her mind was…*what are the chances of another serendipitous meeting? Probably not much, she concluded.* With that thought, she decided to attempt at *creating* another encounter. She planned to call Danny if she could locate him, and ask if he would meet her. Whatever his answer, she would accept it and let it go. If she was able to reach him and he agreed, then the universe was playing its role, and helping with her decision.

Chapter 37

1999 - Reunion on Cape Cod

While staying at a lovely resort, overlooking the bay, she garnered a phone book hoping she might find Danny listed. It seemed like a stroke of luck when his name seemed to jump off the page. But, would she have the nerve to make the call? Deciding to go ahead with the call she thought, *what do I have to lose*? Hesitating, she wondered if calling him at his home could put him in an awkward situation, and she certainly did not want to do that. Instead, she elected to do some research on the Internet, where she learned his place of business and decided to call him there.

"Danny Corrao, please." "Just a moment," came the voice on the other end of the phone and then suddenly… "This is Danny." When Amanda heard his voice, her words seemed to stick in her throat. A moment passed and finally she spoke. "Danny, this is Amanda. I know it has been a number of years since we met on the ferry, and I do remember that you are married. However, I am staying on the Cape and I wondered if we might meet for old times' sake and have lunch sometime during the next week?" "What a lovely surprise," he said. "Just how many years has it been, Amanda?" "I guess about forty or so altogether, but only ten since we last saw each other." With a long pause and a deep sigh, Amanda continued, "You have been in my thoughts continuously since that meeting." "Yes, Amanda, I have thought of you quite often, too. I would love to have lunch. Can we meet on Tuesday? I have an easy workload that day, and it will be more relaxed since I will not have to rush back to the office. How about I pick you up at your hotel and we can drive to the coast where I know a spectacular spot." "That sounds great, Danny. I am staying at the Highland Beach Resort and I will be ready at noon." "Great, Amanda, I will see you then. If anything changes I'll call." With anticipation and excitement Amanda replied, "I am looking forward to it."

The next few days passed quickly since Amanda's call to Danny. She relished her solitude and the majesty of the natural surroundings, where she meditated daily. She walked the beach every day at dawn and at sunset, thinking, thinking and thinking. She searched her heart wondering how she would handle her meeting with Danny. Deep down she knew what was in her heart but she also knew she had to be very cautious remembering that he was still married.

Not having seen him in so many years she was not privy to the state of his marriage or what kind of a life he had. But she did know from her own experience that after forty plus years with one person there are always issues, disappointments and a need for something new, if only temporary. They were both very young when they were involved and now they were mature adults, each with their own experiences and life story. She kept wondering, *what was Danny thinking and feeling about this encounter?* Thoughts of what would be the outcome of their rendezvous were filling all her waking moments, and a few sleepless nights.

The weekend seemed to go on forever, and then Tuesday finally arrived. Filling her mind with so many thoughts of anticipation about what this meeting might bring she quickly showered and dressed. After almost a half century she was about to meet her high school sweetheart. Her heart would not stop racing. She was nervous and excited at the same time. *Amanda, you must calm down,* she scolded herself. *Sit down and rest for a few minutes. You need to be calm and composed when you meet Danny.* Several minutes passed and when the doorbell finally rang she was feeling more centered and in control. She gathered her things and took one long, last look in the mirror, to make sure she looked perfect, before opening the door.

Her heart was fluttering as she reached for the door handle and opened it. Amanda looking quite lovely, just stood there smiling. She had aged well and Danny certainly took notice. He remained there momentarily, just staring at her. "Please come in, Danny". Entering, he slowly moved to the other side of the room. She closed the door behind him, and followed him across the room to the window, where he was admiring the beautiful view of the water. Their first moments felt extremely awkward. Then he turned and looked directly into her eyes and said, "You look fabulous! I cannot believe that we are both approaching seventy." "Danny, you look wonderful yourself. Please come and sit down for a moment." After a short period of silence and exchanging some uncomfortable small talk, Danny got up and said, "We better be going, I have made a reservation for us and I don't want to be late."

As they approached the car, he opened the door and gave her his hand as he helped her into her seat. Before he closed the door, he did something that she never expected and was not prepared for. He leaned over and kissed her gently on the cheek. Her heart skipped a beat as she felt his lips on her face. For a short time, they drove with no conversation. Then he broke the silence and questioned her about her life. Learning that she had been single for the past thirty years, he seemed amazed at the things she had done with her life. He was impressed with her career, as well as all the singing and the dancing she had done. As she finished what was a brief synopsis, they were entering the parking lot. He pulled up to the valet stand so the attendant could park the car. Danny rushed around to open the door for her. Entering the restaurant, the headwaiter seated them at a window over looking Cape Cod bay. It was a spectacular day, the sun was glistening on the water and the view was breathtaking. They each ordered a glass of wine and reviewed the menu. After deciding on their choices for lunch, the waiter took their order. They chatted, savored their wine and waited for the food to arrive. Amanda asked Danny about his life. His business life had been very important to him, but he was now fully retired. He explained that his wife of forty plus years had been quite ill for a long time with a chronic disease, but it was not life threatening due to new medications. He seemed to feel a lot of compassion for her. As he continued to talk, he spoke about some of his frustrations with the situation. But Amanda knew from their conversation that he remained lovingly devoted to her due to the many years they shared together.

Then the conversation turned toward some of the memories of their mutual experiences from so many years ago. They reminisced about some of their shared moments as teenagers, and why they had parted so long ago. Amanda told him she had loved him back then even though she had never verbalized it. She reminded him how he had said he loved her and as she did, her eyes filled up with tears. He just looked at her and took her hands in his from across the table. "I know it was my fault that we drifted apart. I was not mature enough and a little screwed up perhaps, back then. I wanted you so much and I knew if we continued that it we might wind up in an improper situation for two teenagers. Something told me that you were not ready for that. I thought it was best to go in another direction. I knew I didn't want to hurt you in any way." "Nevertheless, Danny, I was hurt, and for quite a number of months. I could not seem to figure out what had happened or why. There was no explanation just your sudden absence from my life. However, I never forgot how I felt about you. I can still feel those same feelings today as we sit here talking." "I understand what you mean, Amanda. It is all coming back for me, too. It has been said that timing is everything and I think it just was not the right time for us. I will always remember what you said to me when we met on the ferry a few years ago. *If you ever find yourself alone in life please call me,* and I want you to know that I certainly will. Maybe we might still have a small chance for real happiness at this stage of life, you never know." At that very moment Amanda finally realized something she had always wondered about; that Danny had not forgotten either, the intense feelings of young love they had experienced. With that statement, lunch arrived.

At the conclusion of lunch, they went outside. Her arm affectionately laced through his, they strolled along the dock and delighted in the ambiance and the aroma of the sea air. They talked and talked about so many things, and then it was time to go. The afternoon hours slipped by too quickly, and he would be expected at home. Driving back to her hotel, he told Amanda that was considering calling home and making an excuse so he could stay longer. He called his wife from her hotel to test the waters and she was quite agreeable to whatever excuse he gave her. Amanda had no knowledge of what he told her, but she was overjoyed that they would have a few more hours together.

While he was making the call from the patio, Amanda poured them a glass of wine and sat on the sofa. When he came in from the patio, he came directly over to the sofa and sat next to her. He reached for her hand and said, "I must admit I have thought of the possibility of this moment for so many years. I never thought I would ever see you again, but here we are." "Yes, Danny, here we are two people in our senior years and yet our moment's together years ago seem like yesterday. Remember when we walked to the sweet shop every time we spent an evening together? On the way home, we would stop at every tree to kiss and hug. You used to sing that old song to me...*Walking My Baby Back Home*, remember?" Recalling the sweetness of that memory, they both laughed. "Amanda, I have been waiting all afternoon to do exactly that...embrace and kiss you, but now, as you are this very moment. How would you feel about that...would it be all right?" My only hesitation is the fact that you are married and I am not. How do *you* feel about *that*?

When he did not answer, she just put her arms around his neck, looked into his eyes and kissed him, with many years of pent up emotion. What really surprised her was that he returned that emotion "Can we go lay on the bed, Amanda? I want to hug you and kiss as I would have back then." She did not need much prompting and got up on her feet, took his hand and led him to the bedroom. As she did, she wondered how far he would take this moment. She decided to let him take the lead. Would he feel guilty about his wife? She was not sure. All she knew was that she had dreamed of a moment like this all through the years and now she was living it. She felt like her heart was going to burst.

As they lay on the bed enveloped in each other's arms he softly whispered, "I have never forgotten how I felt about you all the years ago. I guess I have always loved you." Amanda replied, "I think I love you more at this very moment than I ever did." As she spoke, she began to cry. He gently brushed her tears away and hugged her intensely. Then he said, "How would you feel about us making love right here and now? I had always wanted to do just that when we were dating." Again, she didn't answer she just began to open his shirt and unbuckle his belt. That was enough of an answer for him. They seemed to be suspended in a magical moment that they both had dreamed of, but thought would never happen.

They moved slowly which reflected their time of life. It was not quite the same as it is when you are young and passion is moving you rapidly to complete sexual intimacy. Nevertheless, the passion was there just the same…and the love expressed felt extraordinary. Amanda did not want this moment to ever end. They lay there still and quiet for a long time just relishing in the joy of it all. It seemed like any utterance could break the spell and spoil the moment. Most assuredly, any words would not have any more meaning than what they had just experienced.

Afterward they lay quietly in each other's arms just taking in the love and passion of two seventy-year-old people who had finally found each other. Most people never have to wait almost fifty years to express their feelings physically. Lying wrapped in his arms Amanda whispered, "I wish this moment could last forever. Unfortunately, I know it cannot. We probably should get up so you can leave for home. I would not want you to have any trouble at home because of me." "Not to worry, I will be fine and everything at home will be too. And, if I should ever wind up alone you will definitely hear from me, now that I know how to find you."

As they laid there comfortable and relaxed they seemed to doze off for a short time when a bolt of thunder awakened them. It was beginning to rain and Danny needed to be on his way. He got up from the bed leaned over and kissed her gently, "I will always love you and never forget this day." He went to the bathroom to freshen up and get dressed. She just stayed in bed enjoying these last moments and relishing in the feelings of what had just taken place. She felt so content, but sad knowing he was about to leave. She was grateful for the one of the most beautiful days of her life.

She got up and put on her robe. When he came from the bathroom, he took her in his arms one last time. She held him so tight not wanting to let him go. When they parted, she went to the door and opened it. He kissed her again on the cheek, said he loved her, and he was gone. She watched him go to his car from the window. Now her heart was breaking knowing that they may not ever see each other again, unless his life changed.

Chapter 38

2000 -2010 Dreams Can Come True

A life that is just endured cannot be LIVED!

So, Amanda manifested all of her dreams, even reconnecting with her high school sweetheart. The tender moments with Danny, though brief, will be forever embedded in her heart, for the remainder of her life. She remains hopeful for a future encounter, but if that never comes to fruition, they have had that "one brief shining moment".

Music, dancing, painting, her philosophical studies and being close to her daughter and grandchildren, valued friends, and the independence she maintained brought Amanda through some of her happiest and most fulfilling years.

Amanda's new career, now five years old was going well, but retirement was in her thoughts and on the horizon. With a new grandchild on the way, that idea became very enticing, so she offered to retire and be the baby's Nanny. Victoria jumped at the idea to have her Mom care of her new baby. Amanda retired from the world of business and moved to North Carolina to care for her new grandchild. All through the years, mother and daughter have maintained a close bond and wonderful relationship. Amanda's decision allowed Victoria the freedom to pursue her own career without having to put her baby in daycare.

Enjoying the privilege of witnessing the live birth of a beautiful little girl named Catelyn, Amanda greeted her first grandchild, and a new generation began. She delighted in caring for the newborn infant. It took another six years before Scott came along. As Nanny to both children, Amanda maintains a strong bond with them both.

Amanda's marriage to Bradley has given her the greatest gift of life...a loving and wonderful daughter and two beautiful grandchildren, which she treasures as she lives out the winter of her life. Amanda is also grateful for a fabulous son-in-law, who is a great husband to her daughter, and a super dad to the kids!

Life's twists and turns took her away from her dreams for a while. In the final analysis, manifesting all of her dreams, has enabled her to live out her life with unbelievable peace and contentment. Dreams really can come true!

As Amanda continues her journey, she relishes in the joy of helping her daughter with life's tasks, and the grandkids. As an addition to her spiritual studies and practices, she recently completed training and certification to become a Reiki Master. She remains involved in the IONS organization as a community coordinator, has a library of metaphysical and new thought books and attends workshops now and then. Dancing and music are still an important part of her life. Just recently, she has accomplished learning to play the piano, another dream that had taken a back seat until recently. However, unknown to her at the time, a new creative endeavor was about to emerge because of that phone call from Victoria excited to announce what she had learned about Jane and the DuPris Cottage. Now, as this family memoir is completed, it is almost six years later, and another move has brought all of them to Georgia.

Epilogue

The time to open the doors of the DuPris Cottage to our first guests was fast approaching and as I roamed around the big house one last time so many more memories kept coming to mind. Each room presented another memory or different moment to reflect on, from my younger years.

Recalling the summer of 1945, when everyone was running into the streets banging pots and pans, I had come to realize that they were celebrating V - J Day and the end of World War II.

Past events are part of the milestones in one's life, and give us pause to take a long look back to those moments. Reflecting on the joys and sorrows of long ago seems to bring those same sentiments to the present. This story would not be complete and could not have found its way to the pages of a book without my memories and all of Victoria's research. They were wonderful times with the family all together under one roof, during and after the war years.

At age twelve, I never really knew or understood the entire truth about the Last Will and Testament of my great-grandmother, Jane. All the facts regarding the issues between my grandfather and Junior remain a mystery.

During those years the name Junior was often mentioned but not with much admiration. As a young girl I remember him showing up and the disruption that is caused. I clearly remember many discussions involving the attorney as we sat around the dinner table. The one thing I did know was that Junior was not a family favorite and his name was unfortunately always associated with disfavor on the part of both my mother and grandmother. That has all become part of the annals of the DuPris-Simpson-Camden family's history. What I did know was that the proceeds of the sale of the cottage went to William's widow Mary, with a small portion to Junior. With the closure of that issue and sighs of great relief, the family never heard from Junior again. We have subsequently learned that he lived out his years happily with his wife and family.

I have lived more than half my adult life, except for the years married to Victoria's father, as a single woman. Understanding the history of those women in my family who came before me, some of whom I had the privilege of sharing portions of my life with, has influenced me greatly. Experiencing the passing of my mother and father, I came to realize how fortunate I had been to have the benefit of two extraordinary parents who loved each of their children unconditionally. Jack and Elizabeth had dedicated themselves to each other and their children, all through their fifty years of marriage, always providing a happy, nurturing environment. Those months I spent confined to a hospital so many years ago helped me to know who I am, and that I can depend on myself when I need to. It gave me the self-assuredness, fortitude and strength of will, to enjoy my single life, while manifesting many of my childhood dreams. The great gift of a special love and his untimely passing gave me insight into myself. It provided me with one of the great lessons of life. While sometimes difficult, challenging and heart wrenching, impermanence and change are a part of the natural order of the universe. My metaphysical studies have profoundly affected my personal and spiritual growth, and the wisdom that comes with age. I now understand how all of this has embedded in me a healthy feeling of autonomy that continues to enrich my life. I can see clearly now, how every road I have travelled, some that are less travelled by most, was meant to bring me to the peace and contentment that I currently enjoy.

It has become a great joy for me to know that my daughter and her family have now learned some of their family history. As they experience the beauty of the island, they have come to know that their ancestor, Jane DuPris was a woman who managed to find abundant inner strength in times of great hardship. She had successfully survived in an era when women were treated as chattel or property, and had no rights. Surrounded with strong women all my life, I have reared and encouraged my daughter to embody those same attributes. Women have been and continue to be the strength and backbone of all families down through the ages. I hope that one day the attributes of the feminine will be valued equally and in balance with the masculine, and patriarchy will become outdated.

Growing up in the DuPris Cottage and my memories of those years will be with me to the end of my days. I have come to honor the memory and the legacy of this courageous woman, Jane DuPris, my great grandmother. She has become the inspiration and impetus for these written words and it would have been an honor to know her.

And so…the story of Jane DuPris has come full circle and her legacy continues with a new generation. Next week is the opening of the summer season on the island and the DuPris Cottage will receive its first guests, and provide them with comfort, love, joy and music for the first time since 1954. All through the years, "that grand old lady" from an earlier century waited patiently for Jane's descendants to bring her back to life. This new generation, in a new century showed up at just the right time and transformed a stately old Victorian home into a beautifully up-dated and modern Bed & Breakfast, which includes all the shadows and secrets of the past. If a guest sat quietly for a while and listened closely, I think the walls would have so many tales to tell...some being happy and joyous, others sad, and sometimes events thought to be scandalous during the Cottage's hay day.

All the shadows and secrets that were once a part of Jane's life have dissipated. They are part of history. The DuPris Cottage is now a beacon of light on the island as it sits high on a precipice overlooking the ocean, a stately old Victorian completely restored. All the bedrooms have been updated and redecorated, and some additional bathrooms have been added. The large formal dining room, which houses a brand new baby grand piano, complete with piano player, has become a gathering place for all the guests, especially in the late afternoon when complimentary wine and cheese are served and once again, the "Cottage" is filled with music.

As fifth and sixth generations enjoy the ambiance of this lovely historical dwelling, a family tradition continues. The fruits and effects of Jane's accomplishments during her life have traveled through three centuries to future generations. The DrPris cottage that had sustained her when she needed it and became the shelter for our entire family during and after the war years would now benefit her descendants. If only she could, *"see"* through time and know…but who knows… maybe she can!

Finis

Afterward

I have written this novel to honor the memory of my great grandmother. It is a fictional narrative, which is partly fact, partly my memories and mostly fiction. All the characters and places are fictional. Any resemblance to any person living or dead is purely coincidental.

In doing so, it has enlightened me on how the determination and courage of one woman can affect future generations. Living as a woman, during a period in history when the wisdom of humanity was in its very early stages, it took great will power, tenacity and self-confidence to accomplish the things she did. Jane lived without fear of what her fellow human beings might think of the choices she made, in order to satisfy the longings of her soul.

During the mid-1800's, the faint whispers of women were just beginning to be heard. At the time Jane DuPris was struggling to make her way, women like Elizabeth Cady Stanton, Susan B. Anthony, Matilda Gage and numerous others were beginning the crusade toward women's rights, particularly the right of women to vote and participate in the political process.

Because of that movement, during the 20th century, where I have experienced most of my personal growth, women were redefining their roles in the home, in business circles and the political arena.

The United State gave birth to the women's rights movement as early as 1848, just prior to Jane's arrival in 1856. It continued to rise steadily up and through 1920, and again in the 1960's. It is still alive and well today in 2015. Unbelievable as it may seem, women today are still fighting for equal rights in many areas. As women in the 21st century, we stand on the shoulders of so many, who came before us. We still have a long way to go! Unfortunately, patriarchy continues to try and control women, and the functions of their bodies.

I am proud of my heritage and the fact that I grew up in the 1940's and 1950's prior to some of the changing roles of women. I am an independent, self-fulfilled woman of the 21st century. I hope that this story will influence the reader to follow the longings of her heart, and be the most she can be, knowing her worth as an outstanding self-directed independent thinking woman. I honor any man who can be part of this philosophy, and values independent thinking women everywhere, allowing and encouraging them to be whom they choose to be!

Cathy De Anne, Author

Printed in the United States
By Bookmasters